rough sketch

A TALBOTT'S COVE NOVEL

KATE CANTERBARY

Cover Photography: Isabella Antonelli of 2Design

Editing: Julia Ganis of Julia Edits

Proofreading: Jodi Duggan

Content Review: Sonal Dutt

 Created with Vellum

Smart, successful, and sitting pretty at the top of her game, Neera Malik has it all figured out.

Save for the small issue of Gustavo Guillmand.

The artist with a cult—and Instagram—following has a problem and it's not his preference for shirtless selfies.

No, he has an attitude problem, a minding his own business problem, an infuriatingly sexy problem.

They can't stand each other and they can't stay away from each other.

This steamy enemies-to-lovers office romance originally appeared on the Read Me Romance podcast. This edition includes a seriously extended epilogue beyond the podcast content.

For lady bosses who wear orange shoes with all their black dresses.

one

NEERA

__Scumble:__ the technique of applying a thin layer of opaque to semi-opaque paint over another layer, often to mute or dull the previous layer.

THERE WAS another bird on my desk.

A wooden one, but a bird nonetheless.

The fifth bird to find its way into my office in as many weeks.

I'd paid little mind to the first carving. It was a simple gesture, of that I was certain, and nothing more. Wasn't that what artists did? They created lovely things and shared them with people. There was nothing special about it.

But then they kept coming. No note, no explanation. Just one beautifully carved bird after another. Now I couldn't stop thinking about those blasted birds.

I had an idea who left them but I couldn't imagine *why* he was doing it, or how he gained entry into my office. It was no great mystery, and if I wanted answers, I had only to access the company's surveillance network. Snatching my tablet from my bag, I was ready to do exactly that. But my finger hovered over the icon, a beat of hesitation holding me back. Even if I confirmed my suspicions about the *who* and the *how*, the *why* would linger unresolved.

And I wanted to know *why*.

On a better day, I would've set the carving aside and gone on with my work. After spending the past week blocking and defending my boss against every asshole with an idea at the Aspen Institute's annual think tank festival, I had plenty of work waiting for me. That was on top of prepping for a business trip tomorrow, managing four pre-dawn crises, sitting through two waste-of-time meetings before noon, and enduring one unnecessary lunch meeting featuring a poor excuse for a Niçoise salad.

I was behind schedule, annoyed, and hungry.

Today wasn't one of my better days.

I set my tablet, bag, and tea on my desk and marched out of my office. As I reached my assistant's desk, I announced, "I'm stepping out for a moment."

"You just got here," Heath said.

"And I'll be stepping out now," I said, pausing at his desk. "Do you have any idea where I can find Mr. Guill-mand at this hour?"

Heath tapped at his keyboard before swiveling to face me. "The artist guy?"

Swallowing a sigh, I said, "Yes." I caught myself before

adding, *The one sneaking into my office and leaving sculptures all over the place.*

When it came to presiding over the company's rumor mill, Heath was unparalleled in his skill. That was half the reason he was my right hand. But I wasn't prepared to give him fresh material on Mr. Guillmand. Not until I knew why he was leaving birds at my door like some kind of praise-hungry house cat.

"Beats me," Heath replied. "Haven't seen the guy since that first day when he was introduced at the all-staff convocation last month. I hear he likes to hang out near the gardens but I've never seen him there."

"So, then," I started, drumming my fingers against my hips, "he hasn't stopped by? Hasn't asked to see me?"

"Nope."

Heath dug a purple carrot out of the feed bag he kept under his desk and bit into it. He grew his snacks at the community garden plot on the far side of the campus and foraged for wild mushrooms on the weekends. He was phenomenal at his job and knowledgeable about every facet of this company, but he was an unusual fellow. Around here, unusual was the norm. I barely registered it anymore. Quirky, eccentric types were standard issue in Silicon Valley. It often seemed that the people around here leaned into those quirks and eccentricities as if they were required elements of their personal brand.

Mushroom foraging. Cross-stitching. Throat singing. It was always something.

"Haven't seen him," Heath continued between bites. "Do you want me to call over to the studio?"

I shook my head, already moving toward the hallway. "No, thank you." I stopped, calculating the time it would take to reach the studio and garden. I hadn't formulated a course of action for handling Mr. Guillmand and wasn't certain I'd make it back to meet with the chief financial officer and his team as planned. "Reschedule my three o'clock meeting."

Not waiting for a response, I headed toward the stairs. For better or worse, my office was housed in the flagship building, the central hub of activity. It was a grand, glass-enclosed space bathed in warm California sunlight and scented with mossy green. With native trees and plants, and a softly babbling stream running through the atrium, it seemed our headquarters grew up among nature rather than us bending the environment to our preferences. It managed to feel energetic and serene all at once. Not the ideal place for stomping or scowling.

On a better day, I would've stopped to properly greet the people who waved and called "Good afternoon" as I passed. It still wasn't that day. I could only manage a quick smile as I continued toward the doors, my hands balled into fists and my shoulders tight. I was getting to the bottom of this bird situation and resetting expectations with Mr. Guillmand.

I could manage damn near anything—a corporate coup d'état, large-scale foreign hacking attempts, lawsuits by the dozen—but something about this sculptor drove me straight over the edge.

On paper, Mr. Guillmand was exactly the type of rising star artist we wanted to celebrate and support with a year-long residency. His accomplishments were in raw materials sculpture but several of his paintings fetched respectable prices in up-and-coming galleries. He favored striking new spins on origin stories and creation myths, his portfolio ranging from Popol Vuh, the history of the K'iche' people of the Guatemalan Highlands, to the Hopi's Fourth World story, to the Homeric Hymns. His global consciousness made sense. Born in São Paulo, boarding-school-educated in Switzerland, fine-arts-trained at UCLA—Mr. Guillmand was a citizen of the world.

It was said his father could trace his lineage to the French monarchy. At least the ones who'd escaped with their heads.

The man knew and respected culture, and despite his aristocratic upbringing, he lived an unpretentious life in northern Arizona. And his social media following numbered in the millions. It helped that half his Instagram posts featured him shirtless, smiling, splattered with clay.

Not that I'd dedicated much time to studying Mr. Guillmand's bare chest but it was difficult to vet his online presence without catching a glimpse or two. Perhaps more than that.

It didn't matter, of course. Plenty of pretty faces and washboard bellies belonged to obnoxious men who didn't know their place.

And this man, with his lurking and sneaking and bird-carving, didn't know his place. I realized it the day he arrived at the company's campus. He'd been arrogant, his arched eyebrow nothing short of contemptuous as he scanned the ten-thousand-square-foot studio built to his specifications and then turned his unimpressed gaze toward me.

It was a moment, an exchange over before it started, but it burned long enough to leave a bitter taste in my mouth. After that, I'd made a point of avoiding Mr. Guillmand's corner of the campus. Frankly, I had more important matters at hand than a condescending artist. I served as executive vice president and chief of staff to the company's founder. My days were packed with real priorities. The moods of one inconsequential man didn't rank among them.

"This isn't an effective use of my time," I murmured to myself.

I knew this, but I didn't turn back to my office. If there was one thing I did well, it was shutting down problems. I intended to do just that.

The campus was vast, many hundreds and thousands of times larger than the tiny offices we'd shared with two other start-up ventures back before our initial public offering. There were moments when I missed fighting for desk space and electrical outlets, and waging war on anyone who dared to microwave fish in the communal kitchen.

Most of all, I missed knowing every member of the team. We'd been a family in those early days, a scrappy little group willing to do whatever it took to get off the ground. With more than fifty-three thousand employees in offices all around the world now, we were a different kind of family.

And that scrappy little group was scattered to the winds. Most of the original outfit had moved onto new ventures and passion projects. Others left the company courtesy of a swift kick in the ass. Even the man who made me believe in the beauty and power of innovation, Cole McClish, had pulled up his Silicon Valley stakes and settled a world away in Maine.

It'd been Cole's idea to develop an artist-in-residence program. He argued it was small money for easy PR, and I bought that reasoning. I bought it, sold it to key stakeholders, and saw it through to fruition. It was a solid plan, but it never accounted for Mr. Guillmand's obnoxious birds invading my days.

Or his bare chest.

GUS

__Oiling Out:__ the technique of painting a thin coat over existing layers, often to return colors to the shade when originally painted.

I CLIMBED A TREE TODAY.

It wasn't my brightest idea, but I needed a new perspective on the hills and mountains in the distance, one I couldn't gain from the ground. If I was back home in Arizona's Rim Country, I would've hiked until I found the right vantage point.

Actually, no. Fuck that. If I was in Rim Country, I'd be scavenging for stone, clay, felled trees. I wouldn't be sketching ridgelines. I'd be doing something useful, not... whatever the fuck this was.

With a resigned sigh, I brought my charcoal back to the sketchbook. It was another in many pages of dark, smudgy scribbles. Flowers, trees, hills, clouds. Each more uninspired than the one before. If you'd asked me two months ago, I would've said my creative well knew no bottom.

That was before creating in captivity.

When the biggest, most recognizable internet firm in the world announced a residency at their California campus, complete with a hearty stipend, living quarters, and all the bells and whistles, I hadn't thought twice before applying. I never expected they'd select me. I figured they'd see my name, see my incoherent body of work, and move on to someone more suitable.

I'd made it through art school only because I hadn't known what else to do with myself and couldn't stomach working a nine-to-five. I wasn't classically trained, not really. I had no apprenticeships or residencies to my name and I'd rejected that path often. Regardless, I did well and I knew acclaim in small doses. A centerpiece sculpture in the New Mexico statehouse. Several community art installations across the Southwest. Exhibits in San Francisco and New York. A revolving collection featured at a new hotel in Vegas.

I made my way on my terms and that was essential.

But a slim part of me wanted this, wanted the stamp of approval. No matter how often artists said they did it for the craft, we also did it for the love. The adulation. It bit like a bug and the venom hooked you just as quick as it sucked the life out of you.

That venom had me up a tree in Silicon Valley, staring off at the natural world while my fingers scratched out the shape of the Santa Cruz Mountains. The lines started out soft, almost downy. Lamb's wool in shades of green, yellow, brown. Nothing like the Kaibab Plateau or Buckskin Gulch or the raw magnitude of the Mogollon Rim.

But I had to do this. I had to stretch my fingers, translate shapes into stories. I'd draw my way out of the driest spell in my thirty-six years, and eventually, I'd find a path back to the beginning. If I could do that, I'd learn how to create again. Even if I had to do it from inside a fishbowl.

I was betting on this. I couldn't stare at the walls or walk in circles anymore. I had to get out of my head and move my hands. I never went longer than a month without a new project taking over my existence. It always went that way—until now. An idea tickled the back of my brain until it consumed my every breath and thought. After submitting to that cycle for more than twenty years, I didn't know how to function without it.

I would've been rocking in a corner right now, scratching my skin off like a junkie in need of a fix, if not for a voluptuous, whip-cracking executive vice president. One frigid look from her and I felt the fire kindling inside me. *Fuck that.* It wasn't kindling. It was a goddamn wildfire. She brought to mind steel-tipped arrows and lush camellias and a dozen other contradictions.

And doves. Graceful, regal doves.

When I'd rifled through the warehouse-sized supply room after she deposited me in the studio on the first day of my residency, I hadn't intended to sculpt anything. But I'd happened upon some pale birch and the magic took charge. Two hours later, I had a dove in my hands.

Since then, I'd fever-dreamed a small flock of birds to

life. Goldfinch, chickadee, sparrow, meadowlark, even a nice, plump dove. I'd decided it meant absolutely nothing. I wasn't sculpting birds that reminded me of her in peculiar ways for any profound reason. Muses came in all shapes and forms—music, weather, nature, women—and they went just as quickly. None of them meant a damn thing.

Save for the small issue of me gifting her those birds. All previous muses served *me* and my needs. I'd never served them. I didn't intend to change my ways now.

Except...I already was. I was crafting *by* her and *for* her, and that was the last fucking thing I wanted.

I shrugged off that inconvenient realization and went back to my mountain range. I had several pages filled with increasingly twisted interpretations of the geography. I couldn't sketch anything without traveling down a winding path and then turning it inside out. As far as my mind's eye was concerned, nothing was what it seemed.

These mountains were born of a blood feud, rock against rock, one rising up as the other bowed down. The Santa Cruz range stood as a tribute to the victor but also a reminder of its strength. The cost of that strength was in its scars. The terrible, rippled lesion of the San Andreas Fault served as a reminder of the fight.

Everything was a product of a long, blistering history. I couldn't see it any other way.

An airplane sliced my line of sight, its roar echoed by my growl at the interference. I glanced down at the sketch. The page was a mess of anthropomorphic earth at war with itself, line and smudge void of purpose and composition. If there was any vision here, I couldn't find it. Burning the whole damn thing would be the kindest solution by far.

I pocketed the charcoal and closed my sketchbook. "That's some real dog shit," I mumbled to myself.

I ran the back of my hand over my forehead as I frowned at the sunlight blanketing the cloudless sky. Today was the warmest since my arrival in early June, but a hot day in the Bay Area had nothing on Arizona's heat. I missed the wilderness and my place in it, but I could enjoy this temperate weather.

Then, I saw her in the distance, her dark skin shining in the afternoon sun like burnished bronze. She zipped down the sidewalk like a hummingbird starved for nectar. *Oh, fuck. A hummingbird.* "Speak of the fuckin' devil."

Miz Malik. She introduced herself that way, like some kind of prim, old-world maiden.

But there was nothing prim or maidenly about her. She wanted to play the part of the proper businesswoman, but heaven help me, she failed miserably. Anyone with lips like that would. Full, plump, dusky pink. Always pursed, as if she was biting that silver tongue of hers.

Luscious. Rubens was rolling in his grave and cursing the limits of his natural life for missing the opportunity to paint this voluptuous woman.

It was too bad she was so fucking insufferable.

The lady didn't know how to slow down to walk. If she'd ever stopped to smell the roses, I was certain she'd follow it up with a performance evaluation on the quality of their blooms.

But that hair. Dark and silky, just long enough to brush her shoulders. It shone like obsidian and spilled like a waterfall. My fingers itched to stroke those strands, feel it sliding between my fingers, carve an ode to it in stone.

I should've stayed in the tree. I should've kept my distance. Should've drunk in the sight of her and then attacked some wood.

I didn't.

Instead, I swung down from the tree and landed on the grass with a thud. "Good afternoon, Miz Malik."

The simple black dress she wore, the one designed for the singular purpose of showcasing her hips, defined entrapment. I couldn't stop myself from tracing the lines of her body with my gaze. I figured the dress hailed from a boutique for serious, reserved businesswomen, a shop that knew only the coolest hues of the color wheel. She didn't look serious or reserved. She looked like loosely restrained sin and the shiny persimmon shoes she wore only validated that. There was brightness and warmth inside her, but she kept it on a leash.

"What brings you out of the ivory tower?" I swiveled my head from side to side. "And where are your minions?"

She skittered to a stop, her hand pressed to her chest as she blinked between me and the tree.

"I—pardon me." She gestured to the oak. "Did you climb that tree, Mr. Guillmand?"

I tucked my sketchbook under my arm, dipped my hands into my pockets. "Yes, Miz Malik, I sure did."

She shook her head in tiny, tiny movements. All hummingbird. "Yes and—why?"

"Why not?" I shrugged. "What are trees for if not getting a look at the world from their vantage point?"

She shifted the hand on her chest to her forehead, murmuring, "That's a logical fallacy."

I turned away, wandering over the grass as she stared after me. "You never did answer my question," I called. She huffed out a snarl as I continued walking. "What are you doing out here on a nice day when you could be inside with the machines?"

I sensed her staring after me, a hot, unyielding glare. Here I was, walking away from her when most people devoured every word and bent eyebrow she offered. It was several minutes—excruciating minutes—before she abandoned the structure and comfort of the sidewalk, but even as the grass rustled under her steps, I still felt the heat of her gaze.

"And what are you doing out here when you could be in your studio? The one we designed to your exacting specifications, sir?"

On the other edge of this knoll sat a cluster of yucca and sacred datura. Like anything truly wild, they grew in disorderly clumps. I wanted to explore the ways they attracted and repelled each other and I wanted Miz Malik to follow me. I wanted her to see this because it was real and true and—fuck me—she needed some of that in her life. I couldn't say how I knew that but I did, as well as I knew I wanted her knees stained with grass, and dirt under her nails, and her dress—that proper, boring dress—ripped and wrinkled in the best ways.

As she came to a halt beside me, she announced, "I'd like to speak with you."

Her hands were on her hips and her lips were pulled tight, and goddamn me, I wanted to taste the cove where her neck met her shoulder. I couldn't pretend I'd be satisfied with one taste. Somehow, in the convoluted maze of human consciousness, I was able to find her desirable and aggravating all at once.

I wanted to fuck her and then I wanted to tell her to fuck off.

"Go ahead," I answered, my attention squarely on the yucca. "Speak."

"Would it be too much trouble for you to look at me while I speak?"

With all the impatience in my body, I shifted to face her. "Go on, Miz Malik," I drawled, an eyeroll tossed in for good measure. "You have my full attention."

She nodded in response, piercing me with another sharp stare. "I'm curious, Mr. Guillmand—"

"Gus, please," I interrupted.

"Gus," she repeated with a sigh, her shoulders rising and falling at the concession.

"Why are you so formal? No one else around here insists on the Mister and Ms. business. Should I curtsy too? Is that how you'd like me?"

She offered no reaction beyond a slow blink and that only agitated me further. This woman. She only bit so much of my bait.

"Mr. Gui—I mean, Gus," she said, her eyes fluttering shut as she corrected herself. "From what I hear, you aren't spending much time in your studio. Is there an issue with the space?"

"It's fine. Is there an issue with me spending time outside the studio or am I required to stay at my desk all day like the other worker bees?"

She waved at the open space around us. "By all means, enjoy the grounds."

"But spend more time in the studio," I added, crossing my arms. "Right? That's what you're trying to tell me. I'm on the clock and you want me churning out one masterpiece after another while the citizens of this strange corporate colony watch. You don't want an artist-in-residence, you want a dancing monkey."

"There is nothing further from the truth, Mr. Guillmand," she snapped, slicing her hand through the air as she spoke. "We appreciate and admire your talent. We want you to be comfortable. Even if that means spending most of your time swinging from the branches. My only concern is whether you have everything you need."

"Is that what got you out of the office, Miz Malik? Your *concern* for me? For my *needs*?"

"No, that's not the only thing." She glanced at the wildflowers, regarding them as if she'd never encountered such a sight in the hermetically sealed existence she called life. "I'm curious why you've gone out of your way to leave birds in my office."

I took a step toward her. "Is there a problem?"

She took a step toward me. "Is there a point?"

"Isn't that what I'm supposed to do here?" I stared

down into her coffee-dark eyes. "Bring art to the people. Wasn't that the high-level objective of this gig?"

Another slow blink up at me, and then, "You are not required to literally deliver art to individual staff members. I apologize if that was unclear."

I scratched the back of my neck, humming. "Ah. I see. My misunderstanding."

"Very well."

Her gaze was locked on my eyes, but for a split second it flitted to my lips. It was nothing more than a glimpse but it struck me like a challenge—and an opening. Without allowing myself time to examine my actions, I reached out and curled my hand around her elbow. Heat coursed through me, a flash of fire a thousand times more powerful than anything else in the world.

She glanced down at my hold on her arm, up at me. "I'll leave the birds with my assistant. I'll ask him to work with the appropriate teams to get the pieces on display. If you need any help gathering the others—or whatever you've given staff members—we'll allocate someone with extra capacity this week."

She didn't know. She was the only one and she didn't know.

She gazed at my grip on her arm again, then over my shoulder, toward the office buildings. "Now that we've cleared these matters up, I'll be on my way."

I didn't get a chance to reply. She shook out of my hold and walked off with her persimmon shoes and plump lips, and didn't grant me even a passing glance.

This fucking woman.

three

NEERA

***Anamorphosis:** a visual perspective technique that yields a distorted image of the work's subject when viewed from the typical viewpoint. However, it is employed such that when viewed from a specific angle, or reflected in a curved mirror, the distortion disappears and the image in the picture appears as expected.*

I WASN'T one for knocking knees. I didn't wobble, I didn't waver. Few things struck fear in me.

But it wasn't fear that had me marching away from Gus Guillmand on unsteady feet. No, it was anger. True, kettle-whistling anger. That man was infuriating with his tree-climbing and word-twisting. It was anger and it was exasperation too. I wore a lot of hats around here, but riding herd on the artist-in-residence wasn't supposed to be one of them.

It was anger and exasperation, and an unwelcome jolt of attraction. That wouldn't do. I would *not*. I couldn't lust after someone like Mr. Guillmand, someone insufferable and argumentative and—and distressingly sexy.

I *could*, but I wouldn't.

It was anger, exasperation, attraction—rather unwelcomed—and a complete inability to focus on my work for more than three and a half minutes that had me clicking my online profile to *out of office* and packing my things well before my regular quitting time.

I told Heath I had some personal business to handle this afternoon and he smiled and nodded while munching a dandelion—leaf, stem, and flower. If I was a betting woman, I'd say the office would be brimming with theories as to whether I was leaving—whether by new employment or terminal illness—before tomorrow morning's first chai.

I tucked my hair back, put my earbuds in, and clicked on a podcast before boarding the company's commuter bus. Around here—and other civilized parts of the world—earbuds served as a clear Do Not Disturb sign. Today, it saved me from collegial conversation and mulling over my unlikely reaction to Mr. Guillmand.

Except I couldn't stop thinking about him. His grasp on my arm throbbed like a burn and I was hot everywhere. Our conversations were stuck on repeat in my mind. For the first time in my professional life, I was doubting the way I handled a situation. It was unclear to me how I could've better handled Mr. Guillmand, although one corner of my mind had *ideas* about *handling* him.

When the bus rolled into the Redwood City station, I'd

resolved nothing. I was tired from all the emotional foot-work and frustrated with myself for allowing the issue to consume this much of my day when topics of far greater value demanded my attention.

I tapped open a car service app as my colleagues disembarked. I was a ten minute walk from home but that wasn't where I wanted to go. I was in need of calm and comfort—and a mental reset—and right now, that meant crossing a bridge and crawling along the 580 toward West Berkeley.

———

THE CAFETERIA-STYLE RESTAURANT reminded me of Penn Station at rush hour. It was unbeliev-ably loud and the crowd seemed to move as a collective body, swarming the front counter, surging toward open seats, scrambling to collect trays piled high with authentic Indian street food.

I loved it.

I gained as much peace from the atmosphere as I did the food. Perhaps that was a product of this great crowd and the anonymity that came with it. No one cared about me, my title, my connections, not when there was a fresh order of gulab jamun waiting for them.

I enjoyed my work and I was comfortable in my role but it was refreshing to live a moment or two without those pieces preceding me. *Yes*, that was it. Some comfort food and a reprieve from the world I managed, that was what I needed. Today's loss of equilibrium was a result of a busy week on top of a travel-heavy month on top of a turbulent year.

Mr. Guillmand was the unlikely product of my overdue need for some intense self-care. Nothing more.

One of the clerks behind the counter raised her hand, signaling for another customer. The waiting crowd heaved forward and an elbow connected with my upper arm. I covered the sting with my palm as I glanced to the side, in search of the offending elbow.

But it wasn't an elbow I found. It was a great wall of man, one barely enclosed in a black t-shirt, dark jeans, scuffed boots. One who seemed intent on invading every last inch of my world. I eyed him up and down, arching my eyebrow at his slicked-back hair and clenched hands. "Mr. Guillmand."

"Miz Malik." He loosened his fists and stretched his fingers, then shoved his hands into his pockets. "Of all the curry joints in all the towns in the Bay Area, what're the odds you'd walk into this one?"

"I could ask you the same," I replied, still rubbing my arm.

He tracked the movement, his dark brows knitting together as understanding flashed in his eyes. He slipped his fingers under my palm, pulled my hand away. But he didn't release me. He held on. "I'm sorry," he whispered, covering my bicep with his free hand. His thumb stroked my skin over my sleeve, his touch gentler than I'd imagined possible.

And I'd imagined. I didn't want to admit to myself—to anyone—but I couldn't stop imagining those charcoal-darkened fingers exploring my body. Leaving marks on my skin.

Forcing a smile, I shook free from his hold for the second time today, clasped my hands, and stepped back as far as the crowd would allow. It wasn't far. "It was an accident. Just a bump. I'm fine." I tipped my head toward the counter. "Enjoy your meal. The chole bhature is exquisite."

Mr. Guillmand hit me with a smile that could only be described as undeterred, and he edged back into my space. "Is that your order?"

"Hmm. Sometimes." I shot a glance at the menu board. I wanted a bit of everything. "Don't let me keep you, Mr. Guillmand."

He reached for my arm, curling his hand around my bicep. "Gus."

I didn't step back this time. I let him touch me and I let myself burn under that touch. "May I ask how you came to be here, in West Berkeley, *Gus*? This is a rather great distance from the campus and your living quarters."

His fingers slipped up the inside of my arm as he gazed at me, a curious, not altogether pleased grin pulling at his lips. "Slater Somethingoranother recommended it. The social media guy, the one who takes all the fake candid photos. He insisted I get out of Silicon Valley and he hooked me up with a list of local spots." His shoulders lifted and the gesture pushed the pad of his thumb into my soft tissue. Schooling my expression took serious work when I wanted to moan into his touch. "This is the only one I hadn't tried yet."

"Mr. Wend. Smart man, good taste." I gestured toward

the counter when a clerk called for the next customer. His hand fell away. "Now, if you'll excuse me."

I wasn't excused for long. The neighboring clerk blindly beckoned for a customer and Mr. Guillmand stepped up beside me. We ordered separately but I couldn't stop myself from stealing glances at his profile. The way he flattened his palms on the counter drew my attention to the leather cuff on his left wrist. It looked worn, scarred but soft. I wanted to touch it, to run my fingertips over the raw edge and follow it along the topography of his wrist.

Ugh, no. Why, Neera, why?

I needed to recharge, not gain intimate knowledge of his body. I wanted an illogical smorgasbord of comfort food that would make my mother simultaneously cringe and roll her eyes: biryani, dahi puri, and uttapam, not an arrogant pain in my ass.

And yet I studied the sculptor's big, capable hands and asked, "Would you care to join me, Mr. Guillmand?"

A smug grin split his face, brightened his dark eyes. "I thought you'd never ask."

It was common courtesy. He was a visitor and a new member of the team, and it was common courtesy to share a meal with him given these circumstances. I was being a professional. That was all.

We stood shoulder to shoulder, waiting for our meals. We didn't speak, didn't touch. To my credit, I didn't retrieve my phone and fall down a fake-busy hole. No, I kept Mr. Guillmand in my peripheral vision as I gazed at the pickup window. It was better like this. I didn't hide, didn't prevaricate. I stared down tension until it cooled...or boiled over.

Our order numbers were called one after another. When I reached for my tray, Mr. Guillmand held up a hand, blocking me. "I've got this. You lead the way and I'll follow."

I spent no time considering the meaning behind his words even though I was certain I'd find plenty, instead occupying myself with picking my way through the eatery. Two seats opened up on the end of a long communal table and I quickened my pace to get there before anyone else.

I heard his coarse laugh over my shoulder as I hung my bag on the back of the chair. "Amused, Mr. Guillmand?"

He set our trays on the table. "Impressed. You're a vulture."

I brushed my hands together, glanced at the people seated nearby, sniffed. "What a vivid comparison."

"Like I said"—he passed behind me, his hand ghosting over my lower back, the pressure just enough to send my belly flipping—"impressed."

I sat, busied myself with unfolding my paper napkin and spreading it over my lap. My companion surveyed the diners around us, his gaze settling on the quartet of junior associates beside us from the venture capital firm Koos Blacke. They'd kept up their conversation about this fall's bonito run but made no attempt to hide their eaves-dropping.

That was how I knew they were junior associates. Full associates and partners had perfected the art of invisible information gathering. Not that this meal offered information worth gathering, even for the Valley's virulent rumor mill.

"It's curious that we bumped into each other here," Gus commented.

"If you're implying anything other than happenstance, I'd suggest you reconsider."

"It wouldn't be the first time you've come looking for me today," he replied.

"That wasn't my intent this evening." I stared at him, my expression even. "How are you finding the Bay Area, Mr. Guillmand?"

He dropped his forearms on the table, hung his head, groaned. "You can't call me that."

My brows arched up. "And why not?"

His entire body sighed. Shoulders, arms, lips, chest. It moved like a skipped stone rippling over a pond. "My father is Mr. Guillmand." He focused on organizing the small plates on his tray. "I can't hear that name without my stomach dropping to my toes and turning around to figure out how the hell he's here when he's supposed to be back home in Morumbi."

"Is your relationship with him difficult?"

Gus shook his head. "Not difficult. Different."

"I would imagine being descended from the French monarchy does that to a bloodline."

He hit me with a flat stare. "So, you've heard about that."

I answered with a quick shrug and, "Did you think we'd bring you on without an extensive background check?"

"No. Of course not. But I didn't think *extensive* meant three hundred years of family history, and I didn't think you'd take time from your very busy, very important schedule to get my dirt."

I tipped my chin up. "I prefer to know who is in the building."

"Oh, yeah?" he challenged. "You review background checks and CVs for every intern? What about the guy who works the omelet station in the cafeteria? Or the lady who cleans your office? You know all of them, Miz Malik? You know their stories?"

"You're referring to Ido and Marian? Yes, I know them. I can't say the same for every intern as we have more than five thousand of them in offices around the world. However, I make a point of acquainting myself with the backgrounds of the interns on campus."

Gus dug into his meal, his gaze still fixed on me as he ate. Eventually, he asked, "Is this your way of telling me I'm not special, Miz Malik?"

"Do you need to be special?"

He bobbed his head as he speared a few chickpeas. "Doesn't hurt."

"Mmhmm. I see the royal bloodline runs thick with you."

He choked out a brittle laugh. "Says the kingmaker."

Again, my brows winged up. He knew something of my history as the right hand to brilliant leaders, as the second-in-command who consistently helped the first shine in spite of themselves. This man was robbing me of my poker face and I didn't care for it one bit. "It seems you've done some background study of your own."

Gus reached across the table, drummed his fingertips on the back of my wrist. "You like that, don't you? You like when someone digs up your dirt. You like being noticed. *Explored.*"

I gave him a disinterested frown and returned to my biryani. What had I been thinking? What made me believe I could share a meal with this man and his arrogance and —and his hands?

We ate in silence for several minutes before he said, "You found my comment offensive."

"Not offensive. Rather, needlessly self-important."

"And that's an issue for you?" When I blinked at him, he continued, "I've been here for less than two months and I know everyone in the Valley is needlessly self-important. Compared to most of these motherfuckers, I'm Humble Henry."

"And yet you're the only one inserting yourself into my day and leaving a flock of birds behind."

He grimaced, cut his gaze to the VCs beside us. "Forgive me for doing my job in a manner that fails to align with your specific vision, Miz Malik."

I was prepared to volley back but stopped myself. My attention was my greatest asset and I wasn't paying it to this petty debate. "Let's set these issues aside for now. We can share one meal without contention. I'm sure of it."

He blinked at me as if he was surprised by this request. "Certainly."

After a thorny pause, I asked, "How is your meal?"

He bobbed his head as he savored a bite of dosa. "Excellent. Best I've had in—I don't know—years. And I think that was in Mexico City."

"Mexico City has amazing Indian food." I hummed in agreement. "Whenever I'm traveling, I try to sneak in stops at local Indian restaurants. I have an ongoing samosa study."

I watched a warm, cheerful smile brighten his face and crinkle his eyes. "What's this samosa study involve?"

I pressed the edge of my fork into the uttapam, suddenly and irrationally shy about my multi-continent cataloging of Indian cuisine. "I'm not sure whether it's an atavistic desire or callback to my childhood." I paused, studied my tray. "We didn't eat out when I was a child. We didn't have the money for restaurants and my parents didn't enjoy the local favorites. It took them twenty years to fully embrace Lowcountry barbeque. But on special occasions, my parents loaded us into the car and we'd drive to different cities in the area. Greenville, Spartanburg, Asheville. Athens, once. We'd always go out for Indian and meet the Desi people in that area. Even if they didn't hail from the same region as my parents or speak the same dialect or cook the same ways, they were our people, our extended family. And now, well, I just—I tend to judge cities by the quality of their samosas...and other dishes."

He made a sound. A rumbly, growly, throaty sound. Somehow, I knew it was one of approval. "Yeah? Any surprises?"

"I'm not sure about surprises." I sampled the uttapam. I loved these savory pancakes topped with tomatoes and onions. That they constituted a traditional South Indian breakfast mattered little to me. If they were crisp and fresh, I'd eat them any time of day. "There are Desi people all around the world and many of them make superb food." I gave him a pointed nod. "Just as there are French and Brazilian people everywhere and some of them choose to carry on their cultures in the most delicious ways."

"Point taken." He drummed my wrist again. This time, he went to the trouble of dragging his fingertips over the back of my hand and staring into my eyes while he did. *So damn arrogant.* "But I still want to know your favorites."

I thought for a moment. "Albuquerque. Egypt, outside Cairo. Beijing. Then again, there are no bad meals in Beijing."

"Haven't been."

I tipped my chin down. "Now, that's surprising. I figured you'd gone everywhere worth going."

Shaking his head, he said, "South and Central America, sure. Western Europe, yes. Portions of Africa, mostly northern. As far as Asia and much of North America, I have a lot of ground to cover. I don't know much outside the Southwest."

I pointed my fork at him. It was rude but I found myself wanting to be rude with him, just a bit. "You don't have an accent."

He pressed his tongue to the inside of his cheek. "Neither do you."

"I'm American. I grew up here." I waved at the table. "Not California, but South Carolina."

"Doesn't South Carolina saddle its progeny with a loose-tongued twang?"

I thought back to my pre-college self. Before Stanford, the Bay Area, and Silicon Valley stripped the South from me. Not that I missed it. South Carolina was the place my parents lived but it wasn't fundamental to my identity the way some of my peers held California or Colorado or Texas fundamental to their identities.

"Some. Doesn't Brazil do something of the same?"

"No twang with the Portuguese, *fofinho*." He chuckled, drew his index finger over my knuckles. "Whichever accent I had, I lost at boarding school."

I watched as he dragged a bit of naan through the remains of several dishes, blurring all sauces and spices into one savory scoop. "Tell me, Mr. Guillmand." I grinned as the name bristled over him. "How are you finding California?"

He seesawed his hand. "I got *here*, didn't I? I can handle a map."

"That's not what I meant, you unbearable man."

He shrugged and held up his palms while he nested his leg between both of mine. His jeans were rough against my unadorned skin, almost overwhelming, but I kept that reaction off my face. He eyed the gulab jamun on my tray, pointed. "What's that? They smell like flowers."

"Rosewater. It's not typical but it's my favorite." I tore one in half and offered it to him. He accepted, but not without curling his fingers around my wrist and eating from my hand. "It's similar to a doughnut hole, but for dessert."

He sucked the sweetness right off my fingers and he did it while the VCs gaped at us. More than one Slack channel was blowing up this evening. "Delicious," he murmured, seemingly immune to our audience. Not that I cared much for them either.

"Mmhmm." I gulped back a groan. "If they weren't boiling hot from the fryer, I'd eat them before anything else."

Gus tilted his head to the side, brought my thumb to his lips. "I'd eat you before anything else, Miz Malik."

GUS

Alla Prima: the act of creating a painting in a single sitting, often without any preparation or underpainting.

SHE'D FLITTED AWAY like a sandpiper on the shore. It happened faster than the blink of an eye, but she'd jerked her hand from my grasp, jolted out of her seat, and offered some boilerplate bullshit about enjoying the meal we'd shared and seeing me around the campus but needing to excuse herself right fucking now.

All while the taste of her skin lingered on my tongue.

And then she'd left.

The nonstop crowds prevented me from tracking her movement through the restaurant, but even if I'd wanted to follow her, I couldn't pry myself from this chair. If the heaviness in my cock wasn't enough to keep me seated, the weight of the world as it shifted on my shoulders was.

I wasn't one to process thoughts or emotions with words and I didn't have them now. But Miz Malik's departure left me with the definite sense I'd met my match.

I'd met her and she was delicious.

Slumped back, I folded my arms over my chest and scanned the crowd again. I'd missed the colorful art on the walls when I'd first arrived. I'd been busy gazing at the raven-haired beauty who'd appeared like an out-of-reach apparition intended to punish me for my basest desires.

Then she'd all but purred under my touch and I couldn't stop. Couldn't separate myself from her skin, even as that punishment closed in, loomed large. I'd scraped my teeth over her thumb and asked for it, damn near whispered, "Give me your worst."

I hadn't noticed signs for the adjoining spice market either. I'd noticed nothing but her dark, luminous skin and the way my palms pulsed with the boundless desire to touch her until I knew every secret her body would share. And I still wanted it. I wanted it all.

As if drawn by my true north, I jolted out of my seat and picked my way through the eatery until the crowd fell away and the orderly rows of a small grocery opened before me.

I found her pushing up on her toes to reach a jar on a high shelf. Her calves lengthened, the hem of her dress shifted up her glorious thighs. The backs of her persimmon shoes fell away from her heels as she stretched.

"Mr. Guillmand," she murmured. She didn't bother glancing in my direction. Didn't look away from the spices before her. "I see you've returned."

"Miz Malik," I said, her name nothing more than a sigh. "I believe you've been caught."

"Then," she panted, trying once more to grab the jar, "come catch me."

One urgent stride put me behind her but it was another step that aligned her full backside with my crotch. My hand found her hip, squeezed that supple curve. I traced the length of her arm from shoulder to fingertip as I tapped the jar. "This one?"

She nodded, hummed.

I retrieved the saffron, pressed the glass between her breasts. Her body stiffened but she allowed another hum, another nod. "Yes," she breathed. "That."

"You're such a good girl," I said, my words little more than a hiss as I spoke directly to the tender skin below her ear. "So fucking good, aren't you?"

"Yes," she whispered, her head bobbing once.

That was all she'd offer. A whisper, a nod. Nothing else. She didn't allow herself much but she allowed me far more. And now that I was here, I intended to take everything I wanted. Not because I was an egotistical bastard—despite Miz Malik's impression of me—but because she wanted me to take everything she had to give.

Hell, if she'd meant to cut me off, she would've left. She wouldn't be here, glaring at spices, *waiting for me*.

"Neera." My fingertips grazed her torso and found her nipple, stiff through her dress, and—if I wasn't mistaken—the hard nub of a barbell too. "Can you give me a single reason why I shouldn't pull up this skirt and taste your cunt right here?"

She swiveled her head from side to side, wiggled her fingers at her side. If my words stunned her, it didn't show. "None that I can think of."

I shifted my other hand from her hip, laced my fingers through hers. I placed her hand on her skirt, over the vee between her legs. Together, we stroked and circled until her head fell back on my shoulder and that hum was a beautiful moan. She rocked her ass against my aching cock. "Don't say things you don't mean, sparrow."

She fired a searing glance over her shoulder.

I had to mentally negotiate my way out of biting her neck for that look. Biting her neck, unbuttoning my fly, fucking her while a wall of spices crashed around us. I saw it in brutal oil paint like the exquisite disaster we were, a field of broken glass at our feet and a cloud of color and scent rising around us.

"Good girls don't get fucked in public." I licked my way up her neck, my face buried in her hair. If her cunt tasted anything like her neck, I wanted to drown between her legs. "Good girls don't let the world see them come."

She rocked against our joined hands and touching her over her clothes was no longer adequate. I needed much more. "You're baiting me."

"You're damn right I am, Miz Malik." I bunched her skirt in my fist, rucking it up inch by inch. "Is it working?"

A laugh rolled through her body before it burst over her lips. "I believe you know it is, Gus."

The portion of my brain dedicated to rational judgment quieted to a whisper as the hedonistic portion let out a primal roar. "Don't you ever want to do something bad, little sparrow?"

She dipped her chin, watching as the front of her skirt lifted just enough for our fingers to meet the damp fabric of her panties.

Anyone could've walked by.

Anyone could've heard her sigh in pleasure as we worked her clit.

Anyone could've watched my cock spreading the plump curve of her ass.

Anyone.

And she wanted it—*needed it*—that way.

"How do good girls feel about getting their fuck in the back of a Jeep?"

five

NEERA

Sfumato: *a technique in painting or drawing where the use of fine shading creates delicate, imperceptible transitions between colors and tones.*

"DON'T YOU EVER WANT," he started, his breath whispering over my ear, "to do something bad, little sparrow?"

I was nodding, purring in response before I could think better of it. And why did I have to think better of it? I did not.

"How do good girls feel about getting their fuck in the back of a Jeep?"

Again, I didn't think. Couldn't think. "I'd enjoy that now, please."

His index finger edged under my panties, between my folds. He thrummed my clit hard enough to cross my eyes and buckle my knees. I reached for him, anchoring myself with my fist tight around his belt. "What then?" he asked, his words rough, strained. "You ride this dick a time or two"—he pinched my clit between his thick fingers and I choked back a sobbing scream—"and then you're done?"

"Let's not get ahead of ourselves. I've only agreed to riding your dick once. I'll see how that goes before planning an encore."

His teeth pressed into my shoulder, just shy of biting the skin through my dress. He growled out a sigh, saying, "I'm parked around the corner, Neera. Let's go."

Gus took a step to the side, one arm locked around my waist with my dress in hand, the other working my clit. "Have you forgotten we're in a rather indelicate position?"

His fingers stroked my seam just enough to fray the last of my nerves. I was throbbing, bursting, *dying* with need.

"Haven't forgotten."

A small laugh tumbled past my lips. "If I'm to exit this establishment with you, I must ask that you release me."

"Is that the proper thing to do? Or is that what you want?" Before I could reply, Gus continued, "Because I think you want me to strip you down, spread you out on one of those long tables back in the restaurant, and fuck you until everyone—*everyone*—knows you're not even close to a good girl."

Without conscious thought, my body tightened against his words. "Yes."

Gus tugged my hand away from my center, sucked my fingers into his mouth. Before I could react to the sensation of his tongue against the pads of my fingers, he delivered a sharp slap—then a second, a third—to my pussy. The startled gasp I heard must've belonged to me but I couldn't process any thoughts beyond the need vibrating through my body. The clench in my core was real, spine-bending pain and I knew I'd do anything, anything at all to soothe it.

"Come now, little sparrow." Gus straightened my dress and ran his hands down my sides, raking his fingers over my nipples as he went. "You might be delirious from the idea of an audience but I'm not ready to share that much of you with that many people. Not yet."

Whether the walk to Gus's car was long or short, I couldn't say. I wasn't sure where I'd left the jar of saffron. The only sound between us was the slap of my flats against the sidewalk and the hum of the city around us. The summer sun was still high in the sky but I couldn't say whether the air was hot, cold, or wet because I was melting from the inside out. All I knew was the aching desire to be filled by him...and to be seen. I didn't want to examine that urge closely, didn't want to uncover its true meaning. But I wanted to feel filthy and depraved and—and gorgeously used.

By him. The man who irritated the hell out of me with his arrogance. The man who invented the art of condescending to me by saying little more than my name. *This* man. He was the one I entrusted with a desire so fresh and raw that I didn't know whether it'd lived dormant in me all this time or it was a product of his presence.

"This is what you want?" Gus stopped on the sidewalk, opened the black Jeep's back door, crowded me against it.

His lips mapped my neck, jaw, cheeks, mouth. The hard line of his arousal bumped against my belly.

A breath caught in my throat and my entire body wavered as an emphatic *Yes* pulsed through my veins. But I steadied myself and hit him with a chilly stare. "Are your eyes bigger than your cock, Mr. Guillmand?"

"You get those panties off or I'll rip them off," he answered, his thumb and forefinger busy twisting my pierced nipple through my dress. "I will rip them right off you, sparrow."

I slipped out of his hold and into the Jeep, intentionally forcing my skirt up my thighs as I scooted over the bench until the lacy purple peeked out. "Yes, it does seem like you'll need to do that."

Gus glanced down the street, rocked back on his heels, and rubbed a hand over his brow as he murmured, "Fuuuuuck."

Then he lunged for me, his hands fisting around the delicate fabric and pulling it taut between my folds. The band cut into my hips, certain to leave marks, but I couldn't care about anything beyond the unchained gleam in his eyes. That was for *me*.

With nothing more than my panties as leverage, he dragged my body closer to the open door. Still rooted on the street, he bent over me and traced his nose along the waist of my panties. He whispered to my skin in a language I didn't understand and shredded the lace in one brutal tear.

When the cool evening air met my swollen skin, a shiver twisted through my body. "Gus." It came out as a pant, as a plea, and he required no further direction. His mouth covered my mound, sucking and licking until I was there, I was *right there.*

Until he stopped.

"No." His gaze skated up my body as my breath came in ragged, heaving pants. "No. Not yet."

I glared at him. "You are so fucking smug."

He straightened, tucked a thumb in his pocket, brought his knee to the seat. "I love the way *fucking* sounds on your lips." He climbed inside the vehicle, slammed the door behind him. "Will you say it again? Will you say it while you're on my dick?"

I reached for his belt buckle, careful to scrape my nails over the ridge of his erection in the process. He let out a howl. "Say please."

"I will." He pushed his jeans down once the belt and button-fly were loose. No underwear for Mr. Guillmand. With his hard cock in hand, he stared down at me. "I'll say, 'Please, Neera, get on my dick and ride it like you own it.'" He stroked his hand down his length once, twice, and then settled in the center of the bench seat. He patted his thighs and beckoned to me. "Now, sparrow."

I skimmed the ruined panties down my legs and crawled onto Gus's lap—as much as any full-figured adult woman could crawl in a back seat. I leaned against him, my back to his chest. His hands found my waist as I reached for his cock, dragged it through my slit. His answering growl was everything I needed to sink down onto him.

"Jesus. Fuck. Neera. Fuck." His fingertips brushed the

tender skin below my belly button, moving back and forth. "*Fuck*, Neera, this cunt is going to kill me."

I found my balance by gripping the front seats but I couldn't find my breath. Not when I was full beyond belief. "Fine way to die," I managed.

"The finest, Miz Malik." His hips shot up, spearing me hard. "Let me hear you say it, sparrow. Tell me how much you love riding this dick."

Words were lost to me. They were gone, right along with my oxygen, my thoughts, my contempt for this endlessly arrogant man. All I could do was submit to the commands issued by his hold on my hips.

"You'll say it. Before this night is over, you'll say it," he whispered.

"Does your pride know no limit?"

Using the front seats as leverage, I sank down, grinding against him. Taking him inside me this way brought stars to my eyes. It straddled the line between pleasure and pain, but the strangled cry he choked out was worth it.

"I don't know," he replied. "Maybe you should spend the rest of the night searching for it."

He shifted his hands, sliding one between my legs and cupping my breast with the other. His touch was unbeliev-able, each pass of his thumb over my nipple sending a current of electricity straight to my center. The sounds of slapping skin against the chorus of sighs and grunts and the fireball of energy gathered inside me made me desperate to find my release—and his.

But I wasn't certain I could.

My body was enthusiastic about this activity. I was as

turned on as I'd ever been. Gus met all of my most important criteria. The boxes were checked and this was the sex of gilded legends but I wasn't convinced I'd cross the finish line. Not without some additional intervention.

Huffing out a sigh, I said, "I'd prefer you spend the next five minutes using that ego of yours finding my orgasm."

"Look up, sparrow." Gus dragged his hand up my neck, lifting my head from where it hung between my shoulders. "Let them see you."

Two vehicles ahead, a man stood beside his car, his hand paused near the door handle.

He was watching us. Having sex. He was watching us having sex.

He was watching *me*.

"That's it," Gus growled. "That's what you need. Take it."

Everything inside me pulsed, a hard, heavy *whomp* that banished all doubt of getting mine. I was close—close enough to feel the first wisps of myself unraveling.

"He's watching you get fucked, Neera, and you *love it*."

I made eye contact with the man on the street. I didn't look away. "I—I—I don't know."

"You love it," Gus repeated. "He's watching you ride my dick like you were born for it."

"Like I own it."

Gus hummed in agreement. "He's watching *you*. He knows what you're getting, sparrow. He doesn't have to see your tits or your pretty cunt to know. And he knows it's all mine."

I was wet beyond belief. My inner thighs, Gus's hand,

his cock—everything was soaked and slippery. His fingers tugged at the bar through my nipple, twisting it until I lost the ability to trace sensations back to specific portions of my body. Never in my life had I experienced arousal like this.

"Do you think he's hard, sparrow? Do you think he'll get in his car, rip his trousers open, and jerk off with you on his mind? In his rearview?"

I shuddered at his questions. I couldn't believe what he was asking me or what I was doing, but I nodded. "Yes."

He dragged two fingers down my pussy, tracing his cock as it moved inside me. "Should we show him what you look like when you're coming?"

I didn't have to think about that. "Yes."

"Then ask for it."

That quick, quiet command loosened something inside me and—and there it was, fraying like an overburdened rope until I was nothing more than a collection of fine, unbound threads. Like I was the sun and the stars and the moon, everything, all at once. My pulse pounded in my ears. I couldn't keep my eyes open. It felt like sunlight was streaming through my skin.

I was barely able to speak when I whispered, "Fuck me, Gus."

His answering growl was rough in the best ways. "I knew you'd say it."

GUS

Camaieu: *a painting technique where the artist creates the work using a single color, typically employing tints or shades to achieve to this effect. In particular, the painting's subject matter is often rendered in an unnatural color or hue.*

IT WAS ABOUT FUCKING TIME.

I didn't say it, but god help me, I thought it as I wrapped my arm around Neera's waist and plowed into her. I'd waited. I'd waited for her to find her confidence and her rhythm, and I'd waited for her to beg.

All of this waiting meant I was dangerously close to coming like a cannon shot before it was my turn. Traditional gentleman I was not, but I believed in ladies first. And this lady wasn't finished.

"Look at him watching you." I tightened my grip on her neck. It wasn't enough to cut off her air but sent a clear message. *Others can watch but I keep.* "He can't decide if he should jerk his dick right there on the street. That's what you're doing to him, Neera."

"What am I doing to *you*, Gus?"

She rolled her hips over me, pausing each time I bottomed out inside her. She liked feeling me deep inside her and—as evidenced by my semi-violent growling—she liked killing me with her cunt. But this didn't end with her simply getting herself off on my dick. No, I wasn't having that. This woman—this pain in my fucking ass woman—deserved to be taken apart and put back together in all the wrong ways, and I was damn well going to be the one who did it for her.

This was the one thing I wouldn't let her do for herself.

I lashed my arms around her torso and thrust up into her as her walls clenched around me, forcing a gasp and tiny shriek from her. "You know. You've known along. Leading me on with that peach-sweet ass and your bossy mouth. You haven't played like you don't know what you're doing to that guy so don't pretend you don't know what you're doing to me, sparrow. Don't try it."

"I make you want."

"More than want," I answered. I held her close as I pounded into her, unconcerned with whether the Jeep rolled over from the force. *"Need."*

"What do I make you need, Gus?"

Not for the first time, I wished she'd turned around when she'd nestled herself in my lap, giving me her wide, expressive eyes. It would've saved me from agonizing over every shift of her shoulders and bob of her head, every ham-fisted attempt at interpreting her words while I fucked the power of speech out of her. She wouldn't have enjoyed the gaze of her onlooker that had turned her body into hot, purring lava but I still would've made it good for her.

"You," I answered. "I need you, Neera." I'd tried to hold out. Fuck, I'd tried. But admitting I needed her blew it all to hell. If I couldn't ignore that truth, neither could my dick. "Tell me you're there. I need you to get there."

She didn't respond, not in words. She nodded, laced her fingers with mine, and turned her head enough for me to kiss her. There was a lot happening right now—I was coming like a fucking rocket, Neera was vibrating in my arms, some dude down the street was watching us, and my head was full of strange, clingy thoughts I'd never before entertained—and it seemed as though my body was caving in from the weight of it all. Just fucking imploding.

Minutes passed before I could tear myself away from her lips and take stock of my condition. I was surprised to find none of my bones or my internal organs were splattered on the windows. Also surprising—Neera didn't climb out of my lap the second she caught her breath. Surprising but welcome.

She traced the edge of my wrist cuff. "I'm afraid I'm unskilled in car sex etiquette. What is the appropriate next step?"

Always so proper, my Miz Malik. "But you assume I am skilled in car sex etiquette?"

I caught her side-eye glance and responded to it with a smirk.

She closed her eyes for a moment, sighed. Then, "I'm asking you what happens next, Gus."

That dollop of vulnerability from her was worth everything. *Everything*. "I have some ideas about that. I can't remember eating anything because I was too busy thinking about sucking on your neck. I bring this up because I know I'll require sustenance in order to survive the rest of the night with you. If I can interest you in a snack, I can promise I'll keep one hand in your panties while we eat."

"You rendered my panties useless, Gus."

"Mmm, yes. A fond memory." I reached for the shredded aubergine lace on the Jeep's floor and used them to mop up the wet we'd created between us. "Panties, no panties. You know what I'll do for you."

She tipped her head toward the windshield, where our onlooker was long gone. "Was that...all right?"

I shrugged. "If it's all right for you, it's all right for me."

"I've never done—I've never done any of that before."

"Doesn't make it any less all right, Neera." I kissed her cheek, her neck. "So, are you up for some food?"

She nodded. "I'd like that."

I gave her an exaggerated headshake. "I don't know what to do with you when you're being agreeable. Could you lapse into polite dictator mode for a second?"

Neera cleared her throat, squared her shoulders. "Mr. Guillmand, I'll grant you a short break, but after that time I must insist you revisit the day's priorities."

"Remind me what those priorities are, Miz Malik."

"There are a number of issues requiring your attention but chief among them is seeing what we can get away with in the parking garage at my building. Perhaps the elevator as well."

I responded with a solemn nod. "And remind me which floor you live on."

The corners of her lips crept up into a tender smile. "The fourth, but it's often empty." She jerked a shoulder up. "Everyone takes the stairs. They're busy closing their activity rings for the day."

"As am I." I lifted my hand to her cheek. Her skin was gloriously warm and soft like I'd never felt before. "I won't rest until I've handled those priorities, Miz Malik."

———

HOURS LATER, after refueling at a falafel truck, nearly dying when she sucked my dick in the parking garage but made me wait until fucking her in the elevator to get off, then repaying that favor by putting her Hitachi Wand to good, edge-tormenting use, and then fucking her against a city-view window, I propped myself up on an elbow and peered at her bedroom. "This isn't what I expected."

With her hair tousled and her lips swollen, she glanced up at me. "What did you expect?"

"Your shoes are persimmon, your lingerie is aubergine, there's a barbell through your nipple, and yet your walls are...*white*." I shook my head at the unadorned space she called home. "Tell me the truth. This is where you bring your slam pieces, isn't it?"

"Slam pieces?" she repeated, laughing. "What are you asking me, Gus?"

"A proper lady like yourself doesn't want random hookups at her house, so she keeps a place on the side." I shrugged as I ran my fingers over her belly, over her mound, between her legs. I cupped her there, my middle finger tapping her seam like it belonged to me. Not for the first time in the past ten hours, I considered the possibility it did. That I was tasked with keeping a part of her, if not the whole. "I'm asking whether this soulless box is your place on the side because I can't fathom you living here without wanting to throw a tomato at the wall for no reason other than needing to spruce up the joint. Not to mention, you're the boss of all the bosses and they pay you in gold bars. This isn't you, sparrow." I stared at her navel before continuing, "I'm also asking whether this was a one-night deal for you."

Neera pressed her palm to the center of my chest and turned her attention toward the greige draperies book-ending the wall of windows beside her bed. The reverent stroke of her hand over my heart, the heat of her body against mine, the shy way she hid from the prospect of giving herself over to me. This fucking woman. She was infuriating and exasperating and adorable in ways I struggled to accept.

Most infuriating, exasperating, and unacceptable—she hadn't answered me. The woman rarely spoke without first curating her words, but even for Neera the length of this pause was remarkable.

Something was wrong. A bug in the code, as the computer-y types were wont to say.

Work wasn't the issue. My girl was brilliant. She was the boss. She knew how to compartmentalize.

She wasn't the issue. Regardless of whether she was sorting through a newfound desire to get caught in the act, this woman was rock-solid. She was bright and hungry and devious, and I saw the pieces she'd kept close and quiet.

Perhaps this *was* her crash pad and she did favor a one-and-done model. It was possible. Her nipple was pierced and she let me fuck her in broad daylight while a stranger watched. That she'd prefer casual sex wasn't beyond the realm of possibility.

It was possible but it didn't seem probable to me. Shoving a platinum rod through tender skin and early evening exhibitionism were serious business. They were commitments, and Neera managed her commitments with more righteous competency than I would've imagined possible.

All that pent-up competence meant nothing escaped Neera's notice and she saw everything *I'd* kept close and quiet too. She dug them out, dusted them off, and forced me to take a long look at them. She slow-walked me to the reality that my life was rich and full, but also lonely. That sparring with a worthy opponent was divine foreplay. That I craved the pleasure of being handled by a queen who'd happily behead me.

And she'd done it while being a contemptuous pain in my ass.

It was aggravating—and deserving of admiration.

I would've admired it until her legs were shaking and my name was the only word left in her vocabulary, but she was captivated by the curtains because she wasn't the issue and neither was work or exhibitionism or anything else on her side of the bed.

That meant I was the issue.

That had to be it and...the truth pinched a bit.

"Your silence doesn't bode well for me." When she didn't respond immediately, I continued, "Yeah. Okay. Message received. I'll see myself to the door."

I shifted away from her to fetch my jeans and get the fuck out, but she wrapped her hands around my bicep and tugged me back. I returned my hand to its home between her thighs.

"This isn't my side place. I do live here, regardless of whether I could afford more. And I would like to keep you as my slam piece...or something less ridiculous."

I stared down at her. I knew my expression was cooler than anything I felt for her but I was still chilled from opening my eyes to my emotions and waiting for them to be reciprocated. "Oh, would you? Is that how you want it, Miz Malik?"

With a smile, she stroked the nape of my neck. Her touch was generous, affectionate. *Heaven.* I found myself smiling back in response.

"That's how I want it," she answered. "But I have a question for you, Mr. Guillmand. Why all the birds?"

I gazed at her for a lengthy moment as I shifted between annoyance—she still drove me crazy—and confusion—how did she not know?—and then deep-spiraled adoration—how could I do anything but worship her? "Because you soar, sparrow. Because you're magnificent and free, and I could grow old watching you." I leaned in, dropped a kiss on her lips. "I carved those birds because of you and I carved them for you."

A blush colored her cheeks and she folded her lips together to harness a wild smile. Her restraint was beautiful, somehow bolder and warmer than the grin she attempted to hide.

Then her eyes crinkled at the corners. She ran her teeth over her bottom lip. "Have you ever been to Maine?"

"I haven't. That's—that's the East Coast, yes?"

She bobbed her head once. "Northeast."

"Ah." I sanded my knuckles over my stubbled chin. "Is that where you stable your slam pieces for safekeeping?"

Without batting an eye, she asked, "And if it is?"

"Then I'll pack my bags."

Her brows arched up. "My boss lives in Maine. I fly out there once a month. I'm due to leave in the"—she glanced at the clock, huffed out a quick laugh—"in a few hours. Perhaps you'd like to join me. I imagine you'll enjoy the seaside village where Cole and his husband make their home. Lots of trees to climb."

"You mock me and my process."

"I believe you've mocked my—what did you call it?—polite dictator mode," she replied with a hearty dose of indignation. "But I'm not mocking you at all. I fully support your process, Mr. Guillmand."

"You bust my balls, Miz Malik."

She reached between us, past the erection throbbing on her hip, to roll my sac in her palm. "You love it."

"In a bizarre and twisted way, I do." I didn't know what it was about this woman but—no, I knew exactly what it was. Neera was magic in the cloaks of an executive, an exhibitionist, an evenly matched sparring partner. "And you're taking me to Maine?"

A small smile warmed her lips as her hand shifted to my dick, stroking me in long, leisurely pulls. "If you wish to join me, yes."

"Little sparrow, I can feel your pulse on your clit. You're fucking right I'm joining you. I'm going to Maine. I'm going anywhere you go. That's how it's going to be."

Her brows furrowed. "That's a forthright position, Mr. Guillmand. Announcing how we are to proceed."

We. That glorious *we.* If I allowed myself a moment of wool-gathering, I'd be forced to acknowledge I'd never wanted for that *we.* Never inspected my life and came up with an empty space meant for a woman of Neera's caliber —or curves. Never desired permanence, never ached for possession.

And here I was, wanting, desiring, aching—taking.

With a sharp shove, I sent Neera sprawling on her belly. "Yes ma'am, Miz Malik. That's my position." I settled on my knees behind her and gripped her waist, bringing her luscious backside up where I wanted it. My hand met the heat between her legs. I coated my fingers in her arousal, painted it over her back channel before sliding one finger, then another, inside. "How do you feel about my *forthright positions* now, little sparrow?"

Her hands fisted around the white sheets as she rocked back, meeting each of my lazy thrusts. That sight alone made my cock as rigid as a two-by-four, jutting straight at her as if I needed help finding my way home. "Left side. Middle drawer. Gray bottle, hot pink label."

"Well, well, well," I murmured as I pulled open the nightstand drawer and retrieved the lube. "Prepared for everything, are we?"

"I see your brash attitude doesn't concern itself with logic."

Once I had the bottle uncapped, I drizzled it between her cheeks and over my cock. My hands moved as I readied us, but my mind was deep in the cave she'd unearthed inside me. I didn't know it was possible to experience this many powerful feelings for one woman—and experience them all at once. I wanted to know her, soothe her, annoy her, spoil her, protect her, see the world with her—and own every last inch of her body.

"Me? Brash?" I shook my head though she couldn't see it. "That seems an exaggeration."

She patted the mattress blindly until she found the Hitachi I'd abandoned a few hours ago, positioned it beneath her, and switched it to the lowest setting. My cock, shiny with lubricant and my own arousal, throbbed at the sight of her pliant and submissive in every way—but not at all.

Another wave of sticky, clingy thoughts crawled up my neck and damn near strangled me as I pushed inside Neera. If I hadn't been preoccupied with pocketing the desire to drop some heady declarations on her, I would've made a fine mess of us both and come within thirty seconds.

"If not for my preparedness, you wouldn't be fucking my ass right now," she replied.

"That's how it will work. You'll be prepared and I'll pick the positions." My words came in quick, gasping punches as I thrust into her. "That's not going to be a problem for you."

"Oh, it isn't?" she bit back.

"No, Neera. You like me this way." I reached beneath her, fumbled with the vibrator until it clicked onto the next setting. A curse slipped from her lips and it felt like she was levitating. Like we both were. "And I like when you give it right back to me."

I never went longer than a month without a project taking over my existence and though I hadn't known it until now, the same was true here. But this project wasn't a towering sculpture or myth translated onto canvas in the language of paint.

This project was the most important art I'd create, and for the first time I had the pleasure of sharing my vision.

NEERA

Trompe l'oeil: *a painting technique where objects are rendered with such verisimilitude, they force the viewer to contemplate the object's reality.*

Cole: I have many things to discuss with you when you arrive. I made a list.

Cole: But if you ask me about the Monarch Project, I'll curl into a ball and rock in a corner. Fair warning. I'm not ready. It's not ready. Nothing is ready.

Neera: No Monarch. Understood.

Neera: I am prepared for everything on this list.

Cole: That's your superpower. Anticipating the unknown and then kicking its ass.

Neera: Speaking of the unknown...

Cole: Now I'm nervous.

Neera: No need to be nervous, though you should know I'm traveling with Gus Guillmand.

Cole: Who?

Neera: The artist-in-residence.

Cole: Please tell me I'm not sitting for a portrait. I'm not so egotistical that I'd have a portrait painted.

Neera: No, he's traveling with me.

Cole: He's painting your portrait?

Neera: Also, no. He is with me.

Cole: With you?

Neera: Yes.

Cole: As in...WITH you?

Neera: WITH me.

Cole: Should I call over to the local inn for lodging?

Neera: Not unless you're uncomfortable with us sharing your guest room, in which case, don't derail your focus. I will see to the arrangements.

Cole: Oh. No, yeah, of course. Completely comfortable. That's cool.

Neera: Thank you.

Cole: Thank you for allowing me to observe this in action. The gratitude belongs to me.

Neera: Am I to interpret that as you believing I was otherwise incapable of forming amorous relationships?

Cole: I've never doubted your capability. You are audaciously competent with all things. I am, however, thrilled to find myself with a front row view of your personal life.

Neera: We've worked together for several years. You've had plenty of a view into my personal life.

Cole: That's a matter of perspective.

Neera: Perhaps.

Cole: Perhaps you're a closed book wrapped in chains and locked under ten magical spells.

Neera: Thank you for that vivid description.

Cole: Always. I can't wait to meet the lad.

Neera: I believe he's older than you.

Cole: Does that mean I can't refer to him as a lad? Because Owen convinced me to read a book about the Revolutionary War and in Alexander Hamilton's letters to John Laurens, he refers to the Marquis de Lafayette and George Washington as "the lads" and they were older than him. I checked.

Neera: I am certain you did.

Neera: Should I anticipate you at the airstrip?

Cole: Yes. I've told the lads at the tower to expect your arrival.

Neera: It's convenient, I see. Having your own airstrip and air traffic control tower.

Cole: Best piece of land I've ever bought.

I LAUGHED down at my phone before locking the screen. I hated to lean on the stereotype but there was something about boys and their toys. In this case, my boss and the long-abandoned cannery he demolished and repurposed as a private airstrip. He traveled no more than once each month but he kept a full-time ground crew because he loathed the hour-long drive to the region's other private airstrip.

Gus nudged my thigh with his knee, jerked his chin up in question from his seat opposite me on Cole's private jet.

"My boss," I supplied, tapping my fingers on the table between us. "He's rather fond of the runway he's built himself."

Gus nodded and returned to the sketchbook in front of him. It was angled up, away from my view.

It seemed we were running short on conversation today. When night had given way to morning, all of yesterday's freedom and courage and attachment had gone with it. The power and connection I'd felt hours ago was now replaced with awkward rigidity.

I'd slipped into checklist mode when I'd woken, busying myself with reviewing urgent issues and firing off messages while packing for this visit. I hadn't lingered in Gus's sleepy embrace or invited him into the shower with me. I hadn't spoken to him much at all.

It wasn't that I didn't want to speak to him. I kept a tight routine each morning. Cuddling—and conversation —didn't figure into that routine. I wasn't convinced it should. We'd shared one glorious night and I hurt in the best ways from it, but I couldn't up-end the order of my life on account of that night.

Routines aside, the ordered, strategic side of me doubted this. I doubted we could translate our animosity into more than highly spirited sex. I'd doubted Gus's desire to claim a place in my life. More than that, I doubted this hate-filled fondness of ours was meant for more than a weekend.

We were different people leading vastly different lives.

We'd have our fun in Talbott's Cove and we'd burn bright for several days. Then, we'd return to the real world and burn *out*.

I shifted in my seat as the jet taxied down the runway, the pulses of last night aching low in my core. A noise rattled through me as I struggled to find comfort, part moan, part yelp. And now, it was his turn to laugh. My cheeks—my whole damn face—heated at the memories. But I wasn't embarrassed. I was overcome.

"All right?" he asked.

"Very well, thank you," I lied.

"Doesn't look like it," he replied.

"Thank you for that assessment, Mr. Guillmand," I snapped.

"That tart tongue of yours," he murmured.

We stared at each other through takeoff, a silent exchange of heat and knowledge and mutual irritation. As we climbed in altitude, I battled the urge to antagonize him. This wasn't a healthy means of communication, even if it was entertaining foreplay.

Gus tapped his pencil against his book's ring binding while he gazed at me, his eyes narrowed and a muscle ticking in his jaw. My belly swooped in response to that jaw. My toes curled, my chest lurched. His small, almost invisible reaction to me was enough to refill my courage, my power.

That was when I knew, when I truly believed this wouldn't outlast the weekend. Taking this much pleasure in a twitching jaw wasn't the foundation of a solid relationship.

Gus blinked away when the aircraft leveled off, revisiting his sketchbook. Not waiting for an invitation, I watched while he worked. He didn't appear focused, his gaze fixed on the windows dotting the opposite side of the aircraft while his hand moved the pencil over the page, seemingly independent from the rest of him.

From this angle, I couldn't see what he was drawing. And I wanted to know. Was it mindless doodling? Did professional artists *doodle?* Did they call it that? Or was this how he created—without looking at his work? I had no idea.

"May I ask what you're working on?"

He blinked up at me and then frowned at the page, shaking his head. "Nothing." With a laugh, he added, "Oh, that's right. You're entitled to all my work. I forgot I'm on the clock." He mimed checking off a box. "Must complete masterpiece before noon. On it."

"As I told you yesterday, that is not the case." I shot a pointed look at the pencil in his grip. "I asked because I was curious. About your work and—and how you do it. And I can't determine whether your comments are facetious or you aren't satisfied with this residency."

He tucked the pencil over his ear. "You want to talk about the residency?"

I folded my arms on the table between us. "If you'd indulge me."

"You don't want to talk about how I can see your barbell through that shirt?" He glimpsed at my breasts before shaking his head. "I'd rather indulge in the story behind that than anything associated with the dancing bear portion of my existence."

"I take that to mean you're not satisfied with the residency," I said. "How can I improve your experience?"

He yanked the pencil from its perch and bounced the eraser on the table. "You could start by unbuttoning that blouse."

I slapped my hand over his, stilling the pencil. "Give me five minutes of serious conversation and then I'll play your game for the remainder of the flight."

"You believe this is a game?" When I didn't respond, he continued, "We're not playing, sparrow. It's not a game when it's the way you're wired. You love our tug-of-war almost as much as you love your structure and goals. As much as I love interfering with them."

I ran the pad of my thumb over his knuckles. "If you know all about my wiring, you should know I don't stop until I've met my goals." I dragged my fingers over the back of his hand. "And you, Mr. Guillmand, are one of my goals."

"You scored this goal," he said, his words rough. "Several times over."

"Which means I've earned the right to know why you aren't pleased with this arrangement. With your residency," I added.

"The residency is fine. It's terrible but it's also fine." He turned his palm over, lacing my fingers with his. He stared at our hands as he said, "Silicon Valley is a man-made world. The lines between authentic and artifice are almost invisible and I can't wander here. I can't get lost. I hadn't realized that before coming here. I should've known but I didn't."

"I don't understand," I said. "Why do you want to get lost?"

As if it was the most obvious conclusion in the world, he replied, "That's how I find things."

"Is that why you climbed the tree?"

He laughed. "You're fixated on this tree, sparrow."

"Is it?"

He glanced up, met my gaze. "Yeah," he answered. "That's why I climbed the tree. I was trying to find something real." He paused, gifting me a warm grin. "And I did. I found you."

"I believe *I* found *you*," I replied. "How can I help you—what was it?—wander? How can I help you wander, Gus?" When he only blinked at me, I continued. "You might boil my last drops of patience, but I still want to help you succeed. Helping other people do their best work is *my* best work."

That grin morphed into a deep, full smile. "Wandering can't be helped," he replied. "Back home, I'd follow the land, the trees, the rivers and streams. I didn't plan where I was going or what I wanted to see. No goals, no structure. No thinking more than a few steps ahead. Definitely not management coaching."

"That sounds..." My voice trailed off as I searched for the proper description.

"Wonderful?" he supplied.

"Overwhelming," I replied.

"Not when you do it right." He knocked his knuckles

against his sketchbook. "I can't do this without also doing that."

"I think I understand the origin of this conflict," I said. "You really do need to wander."

"Do you wander, Miz Malik?" he asked.

I glanced down at the sketchbook and then back up at Gus. "Not as often as I might like."

He gestured around the cabin. "What in the world is stopping you?"

"Having a private jet at my disposal doesn't mean I have the luxury of wandering whenever I wish," I replied. "My time is not my own."

He cocked his head to the side, his brow wrinkling as he asked, "When was the last time it was yours?"

I clasped my free hand around my phone. "I haven't slowed down in an age. That's the pace of things. It's an arms race."

He leaned over, pried my fingers from the device. Set it aside, just beyond my reach. "No, it isn't."

"I understand that's your view of the matter, but as someone who has lived in this world for—"

"Too long?" he asked. He gathered my hands between his, squeezing just a bit. "Too long without a break? What would happen if you gave yourself time to wander, Neera? Even if only for"—his shoulders lifted as he grinned at me—"this weekend?"

Yes, that was exactly what I was hoping to discover.

He traced the inside of my wrist, much as he had last night at the eatery. I felt the same intensity from him—from *me*—as last night. The power, the freedom, the courage, whatever it was, it was back. "Have you ever done anything like that? Like last night? Anything in public?"

I couldn't justify my need to know. Not in a manner that made sense. Gus was aware of the lines I'd crossed but he hadn't matched my confession with one of his own. And I needed it. I had to put this thing—this experience—into a quantifiable structure. I had to know what was happening, even while I knew it would flash and cool.

"Before last night, no. But I'm more than happy to be your accomplice." He dipped his head to meet my eyes before glancing to the back of the cabin. "Are you looking for an accomplice right now? Here?"

I followed his gaze to the nook where the flight attendant sat, her legs crossed and her iPad balanced on her thigh. I tossed the idea of her finding me in Gus's lap or with his hand up my skirt around my mind. It didn't zip through me like lightning, didn't quicken my pulse. "No. Not here." I gave him a disappointed frown. "It's not my plane. Doesn't feel good."

He barked out a laugh. "And if it was?"

"Then I might have a different mind about it," I replied. "There are other issues, but that's on the top of my list."

Seemingly content with that explanation, Gus lifted my hand to his lips and kissed my palm. Then, he popped the next two buttons on my blouse. "There. That's better," he murmured.

By my standards, this was indecent and unprofessional. By modern fashion standards, it was merely risqué.

And yet, I'd enjoyed sex in public places yesterday.

The brain was a complicated organ.

Gus asked, "Now that we have those matters settled, what should I expect from Maine?"

I was prepared to describe Cole and his husband Owen, the charming town where they made their home, and the routine of my monthly visits with them, but I stopped myself. "I believe you'll be able to wander."

eight

GUS

__Lightfastness:__ the pigment's chemical stability under extended exposure to light and therefore, measure of a work of art's value and life expectancy.

I WASN'T sure what I'd expected, but the whiplash of owning every intimate part of Neera last night and then barely owning her attention this morning had left me bruised and reeling. My ego took most of the hits but my hopeful heart didn't get out unscathed.

At first, I'd resolved to back off. Give her some space. It crossed my mind to dodge this trip altogether but the truth was, I needed to get the hell out of Silicon Valley. If Lucifer himself was offering rides, I would've hopped in with him.

I'd done an adequate job of backing off this morning. As best I could, considering. I'd put distance between us during the ride to the airport, I'd ignored her adorable expressions as she'd responded to emails and text messages, I'd kept my hands to myself. I'd wanted to lick her neck and twist the barbell teasing me through her shirt, but I'd done neither. Not until she'd insisted I tell her about the residency. When she'd asked me to stop playing games.

I couldn't see how any of this was a game, but I gave her what she wanted. That was when I knew I wasn't backing off, wasn't giving her an inch of space. No, this woman had me and now she was damn well going to keep me.

We landed at a private airstrip that was little more than a paved road in the middle of a forest and Neera was quick to inform me this was one of her boss's many passion projects. Since I didn't know what that meant and couldn't imagine wanting to know, I shrugged it off.

When we climbed down the jet's stairs into the warm evening air, a battered SUV drove across the tarmac. "That's Cole," Neera said over her shoulder. "Owen's probably back at the house."

Leaving the lights on and the engine running, Cole stepped out of the SUV, arms wide in welcome. A dog poked its head out the front passenger side window and barked its greeting. Cole's shirt was on inside-out and he had smudged Sharpie scribbles all over his forearm.

I held out my hand but he backed toward the vehicle.

"Come on, we'll talk in the car," Cole urged, waving us toward the SUV. "My husband will flay me if we're not on time to supper and it's possible we're already late."

I liked Cole immediately.

After we'd settled into the backseat, Neera said, "Cole McClish, Gus Guillmand. Consider yourselves formally introduced." She gestured to the dog smiling at us from the front seat. "And that's Sasha."

"Thank you for having me," I called to Cole. I reached forward and scratched between the dog's ears.

"Careful," Cole warned. "She'll be your best friend if she knows you'll give her the kind of attention she wants."

I was only partially certain we were talking about the dog with the hot pink lobster-printed collar and not the woman to my left, the one who'd nearly decimated me with her all-business demeanor this morning. I hadn't fortified myself for that, not at all.

"I told you when to expect us," Neera said to Cole as he drove across the tarmac. "How is it that we're late when we landed as scheduled?"

"Not sure," he replied. "There are a number of plausible explanations. There are some fascinating theories about wormholes and rips in the space/time continuum. All valid considerations."

"Would a valid consideration be that you told Owen we were arriving at a different time altogether?"

He bobbed his head as he drove straight toward the forest. "Also possible."

"Cole." Neera sighed and shifted toward me with a conspiratorial eyeroll. As if we shared eyerolls over her boss and his complete shortage of with-it-ness. As if she allowed me to possess enough of her to know her sighs, her glances, her moods.

I didn't. I knew that with crystal clarity. It didn't stop

me from taking her hand and grinning in response. Because I wanted to. She drove me fucking crazy and I wanted to throttle her, but I also wanted to keep her as my one and only.

"I know, I know," he replied. He took a hard right turn onto a bumpy dirt road that sent Neera and I colliding on the bench seat. "I won't let it happen again."

"I'll copy Owen on my itinerary going forward," she said, steadying herself with a hand on my leg. I layered my hand over hers and slid it higher. Her brows arched up and her fingers rubbed the soft, worn denim between my thighs.

"That's nice but you know he doesn't believe in email," Cole replied. "Even though you're late"—this time, I was here for the shared eyeroll—"you've come at the perfect time. We're having the best summer weather right now."

He rambled on about the weather and the work project he didn't want to discuss while driving through the woods like he'd stolen this SUV. If he'd noticed that Neera and I had gone silent, he didn't mention it. I liked him even more.

I gestured to Neera, to my lap, and the swelling behind my button-fly. "Can you be quiet?" I mouthed.

She bit back a smile. Blushed hard enough for me to see it in the evening darkness. And then, shook her head. *No.*

"Not right now," she whispered back, a devious gleam in her eyes.

That's right, sparrow. Come back to me. Come back.

She never stopped stroking my inner thigh. My cock didn't get the attention it wanted, but there were days ahead of us before we were due to board that jet again. I'd get mine. I was sure of it.

"It might be fun," I whispered. Cole didn't notice us. He was going on about the market prices for different types of fish, of all things. "I don't imagine he'll notice."

"He won't," Neera replied, glancing toward the front seat. "But Sasha will."

Sure enough, the dog was staring at us over the seatback, her ears perked up and her tongue hanging out. "You never know, sparrow. You might like it. I know how you feel about back seats."

Neera pressed her face to my chest, smothering a laugh. I stole that moment to drag my fingers through her hair and suck in a lungful of her delicious scent. I'd missed this. Even after a day—but it wasn't a single day. It was a day plus every day since I'd arrived in California. Every minute, even the ones when she wasn't around and I couldn't resent her for claiming my attention and branding my dreams as her own.

No, this hadn't started yesterday. Not by a long shot.

———

IF MY LAST-MINUTE addition to this visit came as a shock to Cole or his husband Owen, they didn't let on about it. Instead, they welcomed me into their home and promptly put me to work carrying dishes to the table like I was an old friend.

I wanted to believe it was a product of their hospitality

rather than experience with hosting a lengthy roster of Neera's suitors.

They made it easy for me to believe the former.

That was good news because any hint of previous men would've driven me to fuck the memory of them out of her on the kitchen table. Whether or not we allowed Cole and Owen to watch was an issue separate from the batch of jealousy I was brewing.

It was new to me, the jealousy. I had few experiences of this sort and couldn't decide whether my reaction was healthy and normal or proof I hadn't completely evolved from the cavemen. It was probably healthy. Completely normal.

Just like carving a flock of fucking birds.

Conversation hummed around me while I studied Neera from across the table. I didn't know how she did it, but she managed to slide between a friendly, almost sibling-like relationship with these men and full-on Miz Malik in all her strict, structured glory. It was strange to watch because I could almost see her settling the chief of staff hat on her head as she responded to certain questions from Cole.

It was strange and I adored that strangeness because I was wrong about Neera. She wasn't a taskmaster boss. She wasn't cold or detached. She wasn't any of the one-dimensional labels I'd slapped on her at the outset. She was everything, all at once, and the only label I wanted to slap on her now was *mine*.

"Does that work for you, Gus?"

I snapped out of my possessive thoughts and discovered Cole, Owen, and Neera staring at me expectantly. "I'm sorry. I didn't catch that," I said, glancing at each of them. I wasn't certain who'd asked the question.

"I believe this lad has a touch of jetlag," Cole announced.

"Jesus Christ, Cole. Enough with the lads, babe," Owen muttered, rubbing a hand over his brow. "We read one American Revolution book and look what happens."

"You're saying I should cancel the waistcoat and breeches order I placed?" he asked.

Still massaging his forehead, Owen asked, "It's a little early to be planning for Halloween, isn't it?"

"Sure," Cole replied. "If Halloween was the intended purpose. I just thought it would be fun to dress up and we could—"

"No," Owen interrupted. "Whatever the rest of that sentence is, no."

Stifling a laugh, Neera said, "Cole wants to get started on our agenda early tomorrow morning. Would that be all right? We're known to take over the table and have some spirited conversations."

"I have a whiteboard on wheels," Cole added.

"And it's hideous," Owen murmured.

"Sometimes, I drag out it out here and move the spirited conversation to the board," Cole continued. "It's better than paper or screens. Easier to scribble ideas and wipe them away when they're shit. D'you get that? You know, as an artist?"

I glanced at the Sharpie on his arm. "Yeah," I replied, nodding. "Yeah, I get that."

Owen shot me a pointed look. "My advice is to make yourself scarce. There's room on the boat if that's something you want to do."

"Allow me to translate my husband for you," Cole said. "The physical capacity of my lad's sailing vessel will accommodate another adult, however, the social-emotional capacity of the vessel is limited to one adult. If you choose to go along with him, please do not expect him to speak to you. Oh, and don't fall overboard. It's only adorable when I do it."

"It's a damn good thing you're adorable," Owen muttered. "And a damn good swimmer."

"Thank you for offering," I said. "We drove through a stretch of forest on the way, right? Are there any trails to hike as an introduction to the area?"

"Trails? Why ever would you need a trail when you enjoy getting lost?" Neera asked, a tease woven through her words.

"You know I enjoy getting lost," I teased back. "But only when I have a sense of the land." I glanced at the windows facing the water. Still darkness glinted back at me. "I'm not positive I could find my current location on a map and I definitely don't know what kind of wildlife I'll encounter in that forest. On this occasion, a trail is preferable."

"Whatever you do, don't eat any wild berries," Cole said.

Owen snort-laughed at that and said, "There are miles of trails right out the back door. You can't miss them." He ran his knuckles over his bearded jaw. "There's not much by way of wildlife in these parts around this time of year. A few woodchucks, a couple of foxes, some beavers, maybe a possum or two. Badgers. That's about it. Nothing noteworthy. It's a good time for hiking."

"You might even find a tree or two to climb," Neera added.

Owen nodded, saying, "Certain paths are better than others. I might have a trail map around. Stay here. I'll go look."

Cole tipped his glass toward Neera. "That means we're on dish duty. Wash or dry?"

"You use an unfathomable amount of soap. I can't stand by and allow that to happen," she said.

"Right, so, I'll dry," he replied.

Neera rounded the table, gathering plates as she went. She stopped beside me, leaned in close, and said, "You'll have a whole forest to roam. How's that?"

"You could roam with me," I said, resting my hand low on her back.

She shook her head. "Not tomorrow. Cole has a list. He grows anxious if we don't address his lists with expediency."

"But some other day?" I asked, hopelessly hungry for her attention.

She stretched to collect a plate from the other side of the table, the movement pressing her breasts against my face. I groaned into the glory of her body.

"Yes," she murmured. "Some other day."

"I'm holding you to that," I said.

She straightened, her arms loaded with dishes and

utensils, and stared at me for a moment. Then, she said, "I hope you do."

———

AFTER THE DISHES were washed and dried, and I'd received an extensive explanation of the local terrain from Owen, Neera and I found ourselves closed up in a guest room. We were frozen in place, the bed between us and our feet rooted on the creaky hardwood floor as we gazed at each other.

I was gradually coming to grips with the fact we didn't always know what to do with each other. It was particularly obvious that we didn't slide between the assorted segments of our relationship with ease, not yet anyway.

Eventually, I asked, "What happens now?"

She studied the quilt on the bed. "To what are you referring, Mr. Guillmand?"

"You, Miz Malik, and me, in this room together tonight." I dropped my knee on the edge of the bed. "If you need an out or an opening, I'll give you one. I'll give you anything you want."

She glanced up at me, her lips pressed together in a sharp line. She was looking for the trap. "You'd do that?"

"This house is small, the floors are loud, and the walls are thin. I can't corner you the way I did at the spice market, not unless you want those two listening in." I tapped my fingertips on my leg as my words simmered between us. "I'm following your lead here, sparrow. You tell me what happens now and how you want it to go."

Her gaze on the quilt once again, Neera said, "I don't want Cole or Owen hearing—or seeing—anything. I know we played a bit on the ride here from the airstrip and after dinner but—but I don't want that right now. Not all of it, like yesterday." Shrugging, she continued, "It's not completely clear to me what I do want."

"You want to be exposed when it's anonymous," I supplied. "And when it's somewhat distant."

She nodded. That quilt must've been damn fascinating for the attention she paid it. Through the open window, I heard crickets and cicadas, water lapping the shore, wind rustling the trees. It was a calm, cool night and the sky was a dark velvet cloak studded with millions of jewels, just the way I liked it. And this woman, the one who had the world on a string and knew everything about everything, couldn't make sense of her needs.

I liked her most of all.

"Is that what you're craving?" I asked. "Some anonymity?"

"No," she replied. "That's not—no. That's not it." She started to shake her head but stopped herself. She lifted her chin, met my gaze. "Maybe it is. Maybe I don't want to be accountable. Even if it's dangerous. Even if it's reckless exhibitionist sex in a car. And maybe...maybe I don't know what it is."

"Then, let me help you find it."

She studied me as if she had to press my words through a sieve to understand them. Then, she held out her hand to me and said, "I'd like that."

I took her hand as she climbed onto the bed. We met in

the middle. I shoved my fingers through her silky hair and tasted her lips for the first time in too long.

There wasn't going to be any headboard banging tonight. No sex toys, no up-market lube. No claw marks on my back, no hair pulling. Despite the possessive caveman in my head who'd wanted to sit Neera on my cock no fewer than ninety-six times today and even contemplated defiling the kitchen table, sharing a bed without the possibility of sex excited me more than anything we'd shared last night.

"Me too," I said.

———

THIS TIME, the jetlag was to blame.

I woke up much later than I'd intended and found the sun high in the sky and the waters of Talbott's Cove shimmering through the lace-curtained window. True to form, Neera had smoothed the sheets on her side, tugged her half of the quilt up, and nestled her pillows against the pine headboard exactly as we'd found them yesterday.

Once I'd checked the time—good fuck, it was almost noon—and posted a sleepy-face selfie to Instagram—that shit was follower wildfire—I made the bed and stumbled across the hall to the shower.

Cole and Neera were in the kitchen as promised. I didn't see them, but there was no missing the debate in progress. I spoke enough languages to get around this planet, but I couldn't make sense of a word they were saying.

While I waited for the shower to warm up, I studied the cramped bathroom with its vintage tiles and porthole window. Neera lived in a small, bland apartment and Cole and his husband had a bathroom straight out of the seventies. The better part of me admired the fact these people lived simply despite their staggering wealth. The smaller, grouchier part of me wondered how anyone with their money—not to mention a private airstrip for their private jet—could put up with a sluggish water heater.

My family didn't know the first thing about living simply. Though I'd never analyzed it deeply, I knew my desire to stay close to nature and make my own way was a reaction to them. They knew it too. Thankfully for all involved, my work earned me enough acclaim for them to regard me as an eccentric artist rather than a finger-painting nomad. Eccentric was fashionable; finger-painters and nomads were not. They weren't going to disown me or force me to eat my Christmas Eve meal in the potting shed, but me finding moderate success as an artist made it easier on them.

I washed and dressed as I knocked around the idea of Neera meeting my family. Traveling with me to Brazil, back home to the Morumbi district of São Paulo. Introducing her as my...as mine. They'd embrace her, I was sure of it. They'd see smart, savvy Miz Malik and they'd think she kept my ass in order.

I wasn't certain either of us were anywhere close to orderly.

I spotted Owen entering the kitchen from the back deck at the same time I came around the corner from the hall. A worn ballcap hid his eyes and the print on his t-shirt was long since sun-bleached away. He gestured for me to follow him around the island. Cole and Neera stood shoulder to shoulder at the far end of the table, bent over two iPads. They were deep in discussion, cutting each other off and jabbing fingers at the devices without noticing either of us.

"Heading out now?" I asked him.

"Been out, up the coast, off to the fish market, and back again," he replied. "My day's half over but I wanted to stop in and feed these two. If I didn't, they'd forget and then we'd have real problems on our hands. My husband is irrational when he's hungry." He pushed a glass of iced coffee in my direction. "I'm going to check a couple of traps soon, if you want to come along."

While I was interested in getting a view of the landscape from the sea and I knew Owen required no conversation, I needed to wander. A boat wasn't room enough to wander. "I want to take you up on that offer," I started, "but I think I'll stay on land today."

He nodded toward Neera and Cole on the other side of the room. "They'll be tied up for the next four or five hours. Go. I'll tell her you're settled."

I set off from the house with a backpack stocked with water, snacks, and enough sketch paper, pencils, and charcoal to occupy me for a month. Due to recent developments with a certain lady, I kept a small sculpting kit tucked into the front pocket. Couldn't risk encountering the urge to carve another bird without having the right tools on hand.

Salt water and forest scented the warm summer air and it tasted like rebirth. Once again, I knew who I was and how to exist in this world. I meandered down trails both marked and unmarked, sat on felled trees until my ass was numb, watched deer cavorting in the distance. I picked up branches and rocks, drew nineteen different renditions of the jagged coastline, walked through the town's picket fence neighborhood and heartbeat village. I stopped into a bookstore and bought reading material on the area's pre-Columbian history after talking with the shopkeeper, a delightful woman who seemed to have several graduate degrees'-worth of information to share.

Armed with new insight, I found a large, flat rock over-looking the shore and filled an entire sketchbook with the bounty around me. I didn't acknowledge the cramp in my fingers until reaching into my backpack for my spare sketchbook. I laughed at my stiff claw of a hand and hauled my ass off the rock. It was time to put the pencil down if I wanted use of this hand later—which I did.

I respected the hell out of Neera's boundaries and limits. I also respected my cock's desire to get inside her many more times before returning to California.

I picked my way through the woods and along the shoreline, collecting stones and stray bits of driftwood that intrigued me. I was busy turning a bit of old, knotted wood over in my palm when I bumped into a large outcropping of granite. I stopped, staring at the rock for a long moment. Earth and moss hid most of it, but the exposed portion angled toward the horizon, rough and harsh and amazing.

I wanted Neera to see this with me, if for no reason

other than seeing the incredible things hiding in plain sight.

I turned in a circle as I looked up at the forest's canopy, imagining the way it would filter the moonlight, the shadows it would cast. The way Neera's dark skin would glow. I wanted her here. Draped over the rock. Kneeling, the earth staining her skin. Would she still savor being seen if the only ones watching the show were the animals and the trees and the sky?

That could be enough for her. I could be enough.

And this place, it could be enough for *us*.

NEERA

Craquelure: the small cracks and delicate lines covering the surface of old oil paintings. These defects are the result of the paint and surface's shrinking and movement over time.

OWEN STEPPED into the kitchen from the back deck, several grocery bags hanging from the crook of his elbow and a box clutched to his chest. "Babe," he called. "How's it going over there?"

"Not bad. Neera hasn't killed me yet," Cole replied, not looking up from his screen. "How was the water?"

"Good conditions. Swordfish for supper tonight," Owen stated, not looking up from his bags. "Brooke and JJ Harniczek too."

"I imagine we're only eating one of those things," Cole chirped.

"We'll see," Owen replied.

I admired their easy exchange of affection. They kept their own priorities and they did it without abandoning themselves or each other. I wanted that. I wanted the man in my life to know I valued his presence and I wanted to express that without setting aside everything else in *my* life to do it.

Cole shifted his gaze away from the screen, settling it onto me. "What else?"

I eyed the list he'd scrawled on the side margin of the town's weekly newspaper. "You have a few items here relative to the board of directors signing off on several initiatives, but we've addressed most of the pressing matters. I believe we're finished."

"Except for my Valley Forge," he replied.

"That was in the winter," Owen yelled. "You aren't camped out in Pennsylvania and no one has captured your capitol and you're not allowed to make any more American Revolution references, babe."

With a laugh, I said, "You mean Monarch."

Cole bobbed his head. "I fear the Battle of Monmouth is ahead of me."

"I don't understand your meaning," I said.

"He is saying it will end with a stalemate," Owen called over his shoulder from his position in front of the refrigerator.

Cole shrugged. "Something like that. I can see how the product will meet with mixed reactions."

"That's your view of all your projects before you release them," I replied. "You never believe they'll succeed. If I'm not mistaken, you have a history of assigning derogatory nicknames to your projects because you doubt them to such a great degree. There was—hmm." I tapped a fingertip to my lips as I thought. "There was the Shit on a Stick project. Then, the Deformed Snail Monster project. I believe there was a time when I saw something titled Worthless Splooge Sock. Does that sound right?"

On the other side of the room, Owen slapped his palm against the countertop as he doubled over in laughter. "Worthless Splooge Sock," he wheezed. "Cole. I love you."

"You certainly do," Cole replied with a smirk. To me, he said, "Yes, you're right. I struggle to see how my work will be received when I'm in the development and early testing phases. You're correct, but that doesn't change my relationship with this project. I need more time. I need you to create the cover necessary to justify more time without anyone kicking up a shitstorm about me getting slow and directionless now that I'm his full-time splooge sock."

"Oh my god," Owen panted. "I can't believe you said that out loud, Cole."

"What? Neera's family," Cole argued. "No secrets between us at this table." He shot me a pointed glance. "If Neera wanted secrets, she wouldn't have brought the artist man here and forced us to watch while he made heart eyes at her last night."

"I am not familiar with these heart eyes you speak of." I toggled to my email with the intention of drafting a message to the other vice presidents and the board of directors regarding Cole's request for more time. That was certain to be more pleasant than this conversation.

"You know, that emoji with hearts for eyes," Cole said.

"I know the *emoji*," I drawled. "It's the specific instance of Mr. Guillmand viewing me in such a light I'm disputing."

"I disagree with the majority of this conversation, but on the topic of Gus and heart eyes, there is no argument," Owen stated.

Cole pointed across the kitchen, toward Owen. "See? My husband is always right."

"Now, that's something I don't hear too often," Owen muttered.

I closed the lid of my laptop and sanded my palms together, desperate for a change in direction. My feelings *about* Gus and my feelings *for* Gus were complicated and contradictory. Much like Cole's Monarch, they weren't ready to share with anyone else. "How is that distillery you bought last summer? It opened recently, didn't it?"

"I didn't *buy* the distillery," Cole answered. "I merely invested in its startup. I'm a fan of startups, as you well know from the earliest days of launching that Shit on a Stick startup with me." He dropped back in his chair, folding his arms over his chest and stretching out his legs. "The distillery opened last month and it's doing well. Very busy, lots of good press, strong local energy."

"I have a love/hate relationship with my husband's newfound gin hobby," Owen remarked.

Cole hung his head, groaning. "Don't you start on that again."

"Start, please," I said to Owen. "What's the love/hate all about?"

Shrugging, Owen said, "I hate all the time he spends

over at the distillery. He geeks out over the science of distilling and he samples everything. *Everything*. Twice."

"And what do you love?" Cole prompted, a smirk fixed on his face.

Matching that smirk, Owen said, "I love getting my husband back all nice and liquored up." He shook his head, chuckling. "Thankfully, Cole is an *I love you* drunk. Not too rowdy, hardly ever sloppy. But goddamn, is he snuggly."

"It's true," Cole replied. "I am extremely snuggly."

Before I could respond, the door from the back deck opened and Gus stepped inside. He was incandescent. That was the only word for it. He was alive and brilliant and glowing, his skin sun-kissed and his eyes gleaming, and I immediately wanted to lick that goodness right off him.

"Hello," he said, nodding at us.

I noticed several pine needles sticking out of his hair. I pressed my fist to my lips to conceal the broad, silly smile I couldn't restrain. "I take it you found yourself adequately lost," I said.

"More than adequate," he replied, gesturing widely. "The trees—and the rocks, these huge boulders—and the cliffs! Have you seen the cliffs, the ones just down the way? And how the ocean water sweeps into the cove and pounds the outcroppings? I could watch that all day."

"I see you stayed away from the berries," Cole said. "Since you're still alive, that is."

Gus's brows furrowed as he said, "No berries. Thanks for that advice."

"These two are wrapping up for the day," Owen said, gesturing toward the table. "They've passed the point of discussing anything useful and Cole finally acknowledged he needs an extension. Just in time too. I'm getting supper started now." He waved at us, shooing us away. "Stay if you intend to be useful. Leave if you don't."

"Allow me to translate my husband," Cole said, pushing to his feet. "None of us are useful. We couldn't be useful if we put our entire being into it. My husband wants to cook in peace."

I stood, piling my devices and folders. I couldn't stop sneaking glances at Gus. He seemed to carry sunbeams inside him. I'd never seen him appear this light and loose. I wanted to feast on it, savor it until I shared some of those sunbeams.

Owen nodded, adding, "And get this ugly whiteboard out of my kitchen."

"Yes, babe. Right away, babe," Cole replied with a salute.

"In that case, I'll get out of your way," Gus said. He ran a hand over his head, retrieving several pine needles in the process. "It seems like I need to shake the forest off before the meal too."

"Do you need any help?" I gestured toward him but quickly snapped my hand back, pressing it to my neck. Cole didn't bother stifling his bark of laughter at my question. "I mean, did you get very dirty in the woods?" Owen allowed himself a low chuckle and I squeezed my eyes shut at my poorly chosen words. The gleam in Gus's eyes was systematically robbing me of brain cells. "What I'm trying to say—"

"Yes, Miz Malik, I'm certain there's tree sap you'll need

to scrub off me." He stepped toward the hall, waving for me to follow. "Come now."

With my things tucked under my arm, I followed after him. In the periphery, I was aware of Cole and Owen observing every second of this exchange. They'd watched me babble—a crime to which I was never victim. That was a horror show of the campiest caliber but it was a matter I'd manage on a different day. After Mr. Guillmand was dispatched from my life and I could employ some memory-editing technology on them. Until then, I was content—no, *eager*—to follow Gus into the bedroom and I was determined to understand the beautiful energy pouring out of him. I needed to know whether he felt the same, tasted the same, touched me the same.

He flattened himself against the door, holding it open for me but taking up too much space to allow me to pass without angling my body. "This way, sparrow," he said, his hand low on my back. He urged me over the threshold, my breasts brushing his chest as I entered the room. He groaned, closed his fist around my blouse. "*This way*."

Gus crowded me, his big body hot behind mine as I took care setting my things on the dresser. He smelled of dirt and pine and sweat, and never in my life had I considered the possibility I'd favor that scent. Until this moment, I wasn't certain I knew the true scent of pine, not the artificial one of industrial cleaners and car fresheners. This— and everything else associated with Gus—was entirely real.

He reached for my hand, turned my palm over, and gifted me a small, roughly carved bird. The wood was dry and dark, almost mottled. I stared at it for a moment, passing my thumb over the impossibly precise feathers. Then I turned away, breaking out of his hold, his scent, and set the bird on the bedside table.

He followed, crowding me once again. His fingers tugged the hem of my blouse loose, drawing me back toward his embrace.

"Neera," he said, my name nothing more than a sigh.

"I know," I murmured, shifting in his hold to meet his sharp gaze. I was electrified by him. Not the rush of being seen or heard or anything like that. It was Gus, pure and simple. He was the rush. "I know."

I brought my hands to his muscular arms, backed him against the wall. I smoothed my palms over his arms, his chest, his torso. All that pine and sweat, the hard muscle and warm skin. It was making me delirious. Then, I ripped his belt off. Yanked his button-fly open. Dragged his jeans down as my knees hit the floor. Still no underwear for Mr. Guillmand.

"Can you be quiet?" I asked. He nodded, driving his fingers into my hair. "Truly quiet? Not a sound?"

I needed that guarantee. Even if Owen and Cole knew we were in here and knew we were sharing this moment, I didn't want them hearing the specifics just as I didn't care to hear their marital convenings.

Still, my brain was a complicated place.

"Swallow me right now and I'll prove it, sparrow."

And I did. I took him all the way to the back of my throat. He tasted fresh and vital and earthy, like he was composed of the land itself. I brought a hand to his balls, cupping and tugging and brushing a thumb over his back channel. His hips surged as if my mouth conducted electricity. He dragged his t-shirt over his head, balled it up, pressed it to his face. A noise rattled out of him, muffled behind the shirt. It sounded like a groan, a growl.

The back of his head thunked against the wall as his hips moved faster, falling out of rhythm with my mouth. We kept trying and failing to meet each other, to match each other's pace, but this blowjob allowed for no artful choreography. My eyes watered, and the tears streaking down my face mingled with the saliva on my chin. His balls were heavy in my palm and my jaw ached, and though I'd never orgasmed as a result of pleasuring someone else, the clench in my center every time I squeezed my legs together seemed to suggest it was possible.

This act was a mirror to the moment: frantic, untidy, starved, raw, irrevocable.

I wanted to hold back a bit. Wanted something—*anything*—between us to be simple. What was simpler than a blowjob? Not much. But nothing we shared was simple. It wasn't pretty or tame or traditional. Never simple. It was a fucking mess and I didn't think we knew any other way.

Gus dropped the shirt and whispered something in another language as he gathered my hair in his fist. It sounded like a string of obscene curses. When our gazes locked across the planes of his torso and he looked at me with unguarded desire, I knew it was more obscene than I'd imagined.

I continued working my tongue along the underside of his cock while his entire body quivered.

He continued speaking, the words barely audible and fully incomprehensible.

He twisted my hair around his palm, tugging hard as the first hit of hot, salty liquid splashed my tongue. I swallowed as he hummed, gasped, shook. He gradually replaced those foreign words with my name, whispering, "Neera, Neera, Neera," as if it was equally obscene.

When the spurts ended and he slumped back against the wall, I bowed my head, resting my brow on his thigh while he rubbed the back of my neck.

"You know," Gus started, "I had it in my head that we had hot sex because we argued a bit beforehand. We don't need to say a fucking word and"—he barked out a laugh—"fuck, Neera. *Fuuuck.*"

A tight breath eased out of my chest and my shoulders sagged. I'd needed to hear that. I'd needed to know it.

"Thank you for—" A sudden burst of sound stopped my words. Dogs barking, several new people talking at once, a baby crying. We turned in the direction of the noise, listening as it continued. "I believe the rest of our party for the evening has arrived," I said, still kneeling on the hardwood floor.

"What do you think about this?" he asked. "This place."

I stared at the door separating us from the sound, my cheek pillowed on his bare leg. "I'm not sure," I replied. "It's different."

"So is a silent suck off but I can tell you right now I enjoyed it."

I studied the door again, quiet for a long beat while I eavesdropped on stray bits of conversation. "There's something charming about it," I answered. "Strange. Disarming. But also...charming." I shrugged, busied myself with smoothing the wrinkles in my shirt. "I didn't like it here at first. It seemed antiquated. Slow. Cole was slower too. I'd spent years adapting to his frenetic pace, his surges of hyper-focused activity and him expecting everyone else to move at that pace too. And then...he changed. He came here and he's still frenetic but it's manageable. It's—calm." I shrugged, glanced out the window. "To answer your question, Mr. Guillmand, I do like this. When I adjust to it."

"Me too," he replied, hiking his jeans up.

He didn't bother buttoning them while we shared a simmering gaze that spoke of quiet desires and filthy games. If he didn't fasten his jeans soon, this was bound to boil over. "Gus," I whispered. I didn't know what I wanted but I knew I *wanted*. Needed.

"Hand me my belt, sparrow." When I arched a brow at this command, he continued, "You're the one who threw it. The least you can do is fetch it now that you've decimated me with your mouth."

My palm braced on his washboard abs for balance, I pushed to my feet. I ran a hand through my hair. It was a tangled mess. I knew without finding my reflection in the mirror that my lips were swollen, cheeks warm, and eyes watery.

"There will be no mystery about our activities in here," I murmured, gesturing toward my face. I bent to retrieve the worn leather I'd ripped off him and glanced over my shoulder. "Typical. I did all the work *and* it shows. You—you're Instagram-ready as usual."

Yes, I'd seen his post from earlier in the day.

Yes, it was wholly unnecessary for me to bring it up.

Yes, I had strong opinions on the matter—opinions I shouldn't have entertained. The man was allowed to post all the suggestive content he desired and his audience was allowed to drink him in by the gallon. This was business as usual and I should've reined in my foolish reaction before it spiraled out in the form of catty off-handed comments. After all, I had no claim on him. There was no reason to assume he'd share anything about his bedmate of late with his followers.

No reason. No claim. And yes, I still wanted it.

"Should I step out to give you a minute?" he asked, frowning. "I'll tell them you're taking a call. I don't want to put you in an uncomfortable position."

He could've volleyed back with a smartass remark or a fun jab about me attacking him or rebuke me for criticizing his social media presence. But he didn't do that. I shook my head because the knot of emotion in my throat made it too difficult to speak. I crossed the room toward him, his belt in hand, and wrapped my arms around his torso. "I don't like you, Mr. Guillmand," I said to his chest. "Not one bit."

He pressed his lips to my cheek. I felt him smile. "No, you don't, Miz Malik."

———

I WASN'T A HUGGER.

People didn't greet me with a friendly hug and I preferred it that way.

As far as I was concerned, hugs were intimate gestures. They required a closeness that didn't have a home in the regular course of my life. It wasn't that I was incapable of engaging in that kind of closeness with others or expressing my fondness for them with physical touch. I simply preferred to do those things with other, less familiar gestures.

Talbott's Cove didn't do other, less familiar gestures.

No, hugging was a way of life here. Save for Owen and Cole who knew me well enough to know better, I was subject to unlimited hugs when I was in this area. Babies, adults, dogs—you name it, they hugged.

That was how I came to have an infant latched onto my cheek while also tearing my hair from the roots.

"Elliott, seriously, kid," Brooke Harniczek warned, prying his fingers open. "We can't do this to nice people. Neera's going to think you're a cannibal."

Outside on the deck with Owen, Gus shifted to face me, an amused smile pulling at his lips. He tipped his chin up. I did my best to return the smile despite the parents hovering around me and their baby.

"It's all these teeth he's cutting," JJ said, gathering his son under his arms while Brooke freed the last strands of my hair from his chubby palms. "I'm telling you, Bam, he needs more than milk, bananas, and avocado. We should give him a bone to gnaw on or something."

"Jed, we're not having this conversation while we extricate our child from his latest victim," she replied, sliding her finger into his mouth and breaking the suction on my cheek. I stepped back, grinning at baby Elliott as he sucked Brooke's finger while JJ cradled him. Those three rarely separated. It was unexpected—and sweet. "He can have a slab of prime rib if that's what he wants but first, we're dealing with the fact he tried to maul Cole's guest and it's not the first time he's done something like this."

"After all these years, I'm hardly a guest," I said, waving off their concern. I wasn't one for casual hugs and I didn't see that changing, but I wasn't upset about one zealous infant. If anything, he was a fine reminder that I was due to visit my gynecologist for a new IUD. "He's getting so big. How old is he now?"

"Almost seven months old," JJ replied, pride beaming from his deep grin. "Four teeth too."

"Don't I know it," Brooke muttered. "I'm so sorry he glommed all over you. He gets so excited when he comes here. The dogs, the uncles. Everything." She shook her head, only glancing away from her son for a moment. "I hope he didn't leave a mark. Is it okay? Did he get you?"

Again, I waved off the concern. "Nothing to worry about."

The deck door opened and Owen entered, a tray of grilled fish and vegetables in hand. "Have a seat, everyone," he called as he moved into the kitchen. Gus followed, closing the door behind him. "If you're pouring drinks, Harniczek, do it now."

"Already done," JJ replied, pulling out a chair for Brooke with one hand, football-holding Elliott in the other.

Cole, Gus, and I found our seats. Owen set the platters on the table and turned toward JJ, his arms outstretched. "I'll hold this little guy while you eat," he said.

"Are you sure?" JJ asked.

Owen nodded, plucking the baby from JJ's hold. "This is what uncles are for, yes. Sit, eat. I'll give him back when he needs to be changed."

JJ watched closely while Owen settled into his seat at the head of the table with Elliott perched on his lap. Eventually, JJ dropped into a chair beside Brooke, his gaze still fixed on his son.

Cole glanced up and down the table, frowning. "Why aren't Jackson and Annette here?"

"They're moving this weekend," Brooke answered. She glanced at me and Gus while she snatched JJ's plate away from him and proceeded to fill it with food. "You've met them, Neera. He's the sheriff. She's the little one with the curly hair. She owns the bookstore in town."

Gus bobbed his head, saying, "Yes. I met her today."

I shifted to face him. "What? When?"

He smirked. "When I was wandering. She explained some of the region's natural history and pointed me toward several books on the indigenous people."

"They're moving into the new place, Brooke? Their house is finished?" Cole asked.

"The paint is still wet but it's finished," she replied, handing the plate back to JJ.

"Took them long enough," Owen muttered.

"And Nate?" Cole asked, searching the table once again. "Where is he?"

JJ nodded as he sipped his drink. "Nate is moving into Annette and Jackson's old rental."

"Yeah, he's had enough of the tavern's attic," Brooke added. "Something about the low ceilings and tiny windows and the potpourri of beer and onion rings." She glanced back at us while she served herself. "He manages the tavern now that Jed lives and breathes gin. You'll meet him on your next visit."

Before I could swerve out of that commitment, Gus said, "That would be great."

"That kid needs a dog," Owen announced. Elliott was drooling all over his hand. Owen didn't seem to notice.

"The *kid* is much closer to thirty than he is twenty," JJ remarked. "We can't call him a kid forever."

"Can," Owen replied. "Will."

Cole shot an indulgent smile at his husband. "You think everyone needs a dog."

Owen nodded at the dogs seated beside him, Sasha and the Harniczeks' dog Butterscotch. Their tails thumped against the floor as they waited for scraps and attention. "It's true. I'm going to phone the kid after dinner and give him some info on the shelter where we adopted Sasha."

"I'm not sure he has time for a dog," JJ said. "But he loves Butterscotch."

"What's not to love?" Owen asked, using his free hand to scratch her head before moving on to Sasha. "Nate would do well with a dog. He needs someone counting on him."

"How is the distillery business coming along?" I asked JJ.

He ran a hand down his face, laughing. "Better than I'd expected. More tiring than I'd expected."

"Four teeth before seven months is part of the exhaustion," Brooke quipped. "Our kid likes to beat all expectations."

"My wife is correct. If he keeps going at this pace, I'll be able to put him to work pouring drinks some time next summer," JJ said. "Honestly, it's been incredible. We're closed one day per week now and that day is necessary to keep everything stocked and working properly. The real challenge is demand. We have a waiting list for events and distribution partners already. I didn't expect we'd get to this point for several years."

"I'm thrilled to hear it," I said.

"And I'm thrilled to drink it," Cole added.

Owen chuckled. "I'm thrilled you're a cozy drunk."

"How is your world, Neera?" Brooke asked. "It must be bizarre to go between Silicon Valley and Talbott's Cove. When I first came back here from New York City, I was fixated on all the overwhelming differences. I couldn't see the village without noticing the absence of yellow taxis and gridlock. It's quiet and everyone walks slowly and it is so freaking dark at night. Right? Do you notice these things?"

"There is some culture shock," I admitted with a laugh. "But Cole keeps me busy. I barely get time to notice the lack of noise and light when we're working together."

"I'm sure he does," JJ said. "It's not easy to keep track of this guy. I don't envy you."

Bristling, I forced a grin and lifted my drink to my lips.

It was an innocuous comment—and one from a man who knew the realities of working with Cole—but it hit me the wrong way. When I boiled it all down, JJ was right. I kept track of Cole. My career was composed of helping men achieve great things by keeping them out of their own way.

At what point would I achieve something of my own? It wasn't a thought I entertained often. On most days, I was content—more than that, *satisfied*—with being the one who made things happen.

Suddenly, I didn't feel content today.

———

LATER THAT NIGHT, Gus and I were again closed up in the guest room. This time, we were getting ready for bed. Unlike the hedonistic moment we'd shared earlier, this was domestic and chaste. I tended to my extensive nightly skincare routine while Gus cleaned the remains of charcoal from his wrists and palms. I caught glimpses of him in the mirror as he hummed to himself and he circled a damp bit of cloth over his skin, focusing on the stains pressed far into the fine creases of skin.

"Let me ask you again," he started, "what do you think about all this?" He gestured to the door. "The family and the dogs and the baby and the total absence of business as usual. At least the business to which you're familiar."

"Regardless of my previous comments on the matter, you're expecting me to confess I hate it," I murmured. "That I prefer the clean structure of the Valley."

"And all its tightly branded bullshit? Yeah. I am anticipating that."

Instead of answering him, I asked, "What did you think of this evening's gathering?"

Frowning down at his palms, he replied, "I enjoyed it in spite of my expectations."

"Meaning what, exactly?"

"Meaning this isn't the norm for either of us," he replied. "You like your clean structure and I like my wide open spaces, and somehow both of us enjoyed that meal of chaos."

"It wasn't *chaos*," I argued. "It was emblematic of a different phase of life, one where animals and tiny humans are as relevant as the adults and their endeavors."

"Do you like that phase of life?" he asked. "The one with animals and—what did you call them?—tiny humans?"

I barked out a laugh. "I'm very happy for people who choose to bring children into the world and commit to raising them in loving families. My sister Talbia has two children," I added, almost an afterthought. "A boy and girl. They're young, four and six, if my memory serves. She adores them. She was meant to be a mother. She's a good daughter, as well. My parents live with her and her husband. She has what it takes to do those things and she's remarkably successful. The desire to nurture is not one I share."

"Isn't it, though?" he asked. "You gather up helpless creatures to save them from themselves. They aren't infants or the elderly, but you nurture them just the same, sparrow."

I glared at him. "You wouldn't say that to a male chief of staff."

"Probably not," he admitted. "But I only said it because you suggested your sister is the successful sibling based on her capacity for keeping her children and your parents tended."

"She *is* the successful one," I replied.

Behind me, Gus snickered. "You are fascinating, Miz Malik. Paid in gold bars, traveling on private jets, and debating measures of success."

"In her way, she is phenomenally successful. My life isn't meaningful and valuable because I earn a good living"—another snicker—"or travel comfortably. And her life doesn't lack meaning because her days are spent caring for her husband, her children, our parents. But I do know I wouldn't have the same success if I tried my hand at living her life."

"I'm sure you'd make a fine mother," he said.

"Don't do that. Don't patronize me," I replied. "Whenever a woman announces she isn't interested in motherhood, everyone jumps to convince her it's worth it, she'd be a natural, she'll regret missing out on her childbearing years when she's older. That doesn't account for the truth that some women aren't cut out for the task and others simply do not want the job."

"And you don't," he added.

I shook my head once. "I don't think I do, no."

"I respect that." With a nod, Gus tossed his rag to the

floor and reached for my waist. "I know you said you wanted to keep it chill around your boss," he started, his lips on the back of my neck, "but, earlier...when we...*you* didn't—"

"I'm all right," I said, laughing. Talk about conversational whiplash. "There's no scorecard."

He tugged off his shirt, threw it in the same direction as his rag. "Maybe not but I believe in equality."

I eyed him in the mirror, my lips quirking up. "Do you?"

"Indeed. It's one of my top concerns. I don't believe you can be quiet, however. That's my secondary concern."

"What, may I ask, is your proposed solution?"

He shuffled toward the window, bending at the waist to peer out into the darkness. "I propose we take a stroll down the dock." He stood, glancing around the room before yanking a plaid wool blanket off the foot of the bed. "And we're taking this with us. I can handle my share of bug bites but splinters in my ass are a different story."

GUS

***Tenebrism:** a technique employing extreme contrasts of light and dark used to increase emotion and drama.*

ON OUR LAST day in Talbott's Cove, I woke up with the dawn. Neera was still asleep. I shifted toward her, wrapping my arms around her waist. I wanted to hold her close and savor this moment before it ended. I wasn't ready for the end, not in the least. I didn't even want to leave the bed because I knew every step away from this location was a step closer to the conclusion of us.

I couldn't explain it though I knew there was something magical about this town. For me, for us. It was more than the slower pace, more than the forest and sea. It was a place for wandering but also finding. It was roots—permanence—without losing any of the wildness that pumped in my veins. And I knew it was inside Neera too.

I continued to doubt my ability to find this town—hell, the state—on a map, but I wanted to stick around. More than that, I wanted Neera to stick around with me. I wanted to keep all of this.

———

WHY NEERA AGREED to come on a walk through the woods while the sun was still busy rising would always be a mystery to me. Regardless, I managed to get her out of bed and out of the house without attracting the attention of our hosts and that was a gift because I needed time with her. Time and space to make my case, make her see the things I saw.

We walked in silence for several minutes as I searched for the rock I'd noticed the first time I'd explored this area. I'd wanted her to see this and I'd wanted to see her here. It took several more minutes of heading in one direction, doubling back, starting off in another direction, retreating, and finally settling on the right path before that strange, wonderful outcropping.

"Isn't this amazing?" I asked as we circled the exposed rock. "There's so much I could do with this."

She blinked at the rock. "Sculpting, you mean?"

"Maybe but also—anything," I said. "It's marvelous to study. It's a story waiting to be told." I dropped my hands to her waist and steered her toward it. "Sit there for me. Please," I added when she gave me a baleful stare. I shrugged my backpack off my shoulders and retrieved a sketchbook and charcoal. "Please, sparrow."

She nestled on the upper slab, her legs tucked under her and her body angled toward the ocean. "Is this what you want?"

I stared at her, perched on the edge of a majestic rock as if she was presiding over this land. I flipped open my book as images flooded my mind's eye. "This is exactly what I want." Not missing her slight eyeroll, I continued, "I've learned a few things about this land since we've been here. The land and the people who have lived on it throughout time. I don't know those stories well enough to tell them yet, but I want to find my way there. I want to learn and I want to figure it out because when I came across this rock and saw it jutting out of the ground like it'd been thrown down from the heavens or shot out of hell, I knew I had to translate this story. I want to tell the story of this place."

She ran her fingers over the mossy ledge, saying, "I like this side of you. The hyper, driven side. I like that you've shared it with me and...I can't wait to see the story you tell."

Still staring at her fingers as they stroked the moss, I asked, "Will you tell me a story?"

"What kind of story?"

"A story of the future," I said, my gaze fixed on her hand while I sketched. "What comes next? Where do we go? *Who* are we?"

"That's a complicated story," she replied, twisting her hands together.

"I don't think it is." I flipped to a new page. "What do you want to do with your life, Neera? Tell me that."

I could feel her frowning at me for several heavy beats before she asked, "In what sense?"

"The rock you're sitting on has been here for at least twelve thousand years. Probably longer. I stumbled upon it a few days ago and I knew—I fucking *knew*—it deserved attention. It came from somewhere and it served purposes great and small and it's worth remembering." I turned the page, started sketching again. "What do you want from this life, Neera?"

She sucked in a breath and I knew the dam was breaking.

"I want to do something," she started, her voice smaller than I'd ever heard it, "something of my own."

"It's your turn to be *seen*, isn't it?" Another breath and I could almost see her heart swelling with the pleasure of recognition. "That's what it is. Recognition *of* you, *for* you. Not because of anyone else but because you're brilliant and talented and you've earned it."

She hesitated. "I think—"

"No," I argued. "You *know* what you want. Say it. Just fucking say it, sparrow. We're all alone out here. You and me and a rock that's nowhere near as tough as you. *Say it*."

"I want to build something that will outlast me, something that will leave a mark." She ran her fingers through her hair, her lips pursed and her eyes unfocused on the horizon. "I want to get better, more accessible math and science and coding instruction in public schools. I want to make it more attractive to build technology that improves quality of life rather than that objective being secondary to profit and IPO valuations. I want to build windmill farms in developing countries and solar arrays in the desert, and I want to fund midwives and nurse practitioners in every small, impoverished town in this country. And it's not because philanthropy calls to my soul or I feel a need to give back after years of raking in exorbitant corporate profit. It's not about nurturing or any other maternal bullshit that gets pinned on women who put their energy into these endeavors. We need math instruction because we need talent. We need quality of life tech because the population of many developed nations is aging faster than the greater population is growing, and younger generations can't carry that burden alone. We need wind and solar and midwives because those developing countries and small towns represent talent pipelines and untapped markets. We need to create the world we want to do business in if we want to keep seeing those profits. And I want"—she shook her head as if this one was the true impossibility —"I want to make decisions rather than executing on someone's decisions."

"Then why don't you?"

"Because"—she slapped her palms against the stone —"because Cole needs me."

"I don't know shit about the internet—"

"Your Instagram engagement says otherwise," she quipped. "You know how to save the best moments for your followers."

I didn't know what I'd done wrong, but I knew it was something and I wanted to fix it right now. I glanced down at myself, considering my shirt. I pulled it over my head, rubbed a charcoal-darkened hand over my chest, and asked, "Better?"

She tipped her chin down. Her eyes answered for her. Yes, this was better. But she still frowned, asking, "Do you plan on posting a pic of this for your fans?"

"Only if I can also tell them this charcoal is a result of sketching the woman I'd like to call mine all morning. I haven't mentioned it to them yet because we haven't had the conversation and I'm not about to make announcements on social media without your prior knowledge."

"I—you—what?"

"I don't have to tag you if you don't want," I continued. "Business and pleasure can live separately for now."

"For now?" she repeated.

"Until it's professionally convenient for you. Until I'm no longer working under you—in the organizational structure sense, that is. Until you get to work on building some windmills." I turned the page. "Until you let the world see you, Neera."

"And you?" she asked. "Should I allow you to see me, Mr. Guillmand?"

"You should allow me to join you on your voyage, wherever it takes you. I'm a fine traveling companion, as I believe you've noticed."

She considered this, inclining her head in agreement. "You do pack more paintbrushes than pants."

"You say this as if it's a problem," I replied.

She didn't acknowledge my comment, only gazing back at the sunrise piercing the horizon. "We don't even know each other."

"Can you really say that after my cock has been in your ass?"

She ran her hand down her face, groaning. Now, that made for a beautiful picture. My hand could barely keep up with my mind. "Gus."

"Neera," I replied.

"We don't *know* each other," she repeated. "What if we—if we don't have compatible values?"

"I think we do," I said, my gaze still fixed on the page. "And if we don't, we'll adjust. We'll learn."

"You make it seem as though we have a long history of compromise," she murmured. "Which we do not."

"No, we don't," I agreed. "But we have a long history of yelling at each other and being obscene, and that has to count for something."

"It might," she conceded. "I'm not convinced it counts enough."

"Then I'll just love you harder," I said.

"You do not love me," she said. "I'm sorry, no. Not yet."

"But I will," I replied. "And you will too."

She stared at me as if she didn't understand the language I was speaking—which was possible. I'd been known to slip into Portuguese on occasion. French when I was very, very drunk. But I didn't think that was the issue here. No, I was making bold statements and backing them up with nothing more than a foggy belief that this might be *it*.

Eventually, she said, "Your residency—"

"I will complete it," I said with a sigh. I did not want to think about the Valley until absolutely necessary. "I imagine it will take you that long to find a suitable replacement. Rather, ten replacements who will deign to fill your shoes and struggle mightily."

"It will take that long to transition Cole," she said, mostly to herself.

"On that count, we agree."

"And then, what?" she demanded, setting her stare toward me. "You follow me from place to place while I—whatever it is I do in this fictional rendition of the future?"

I jerked a shoulder up, continued sketching. "Perhaps." Turned the page. "Perhaps I stay here."

"And what will you do *here*, Mr. Guillmand? You enjoy the forests and the shore and the dinners filled with dogs and babies now, but what happens after a few months? When you want to get lost somewhere new?"

"I don't imagine I will," I replied. I stuffed the charcoal in my pocket and tucked the book under my arm. "I think I'd like to build us a nest, sparrow."

NEERA

Sinking in: *a condition in which the paint medium absorbs into the underlying paint layer.*

Three years later

THERE WAS a bird waiting for me when I arrived home this morning.

I leaned a hip against the kitchen counter as I studied the newest addition to my flock. This one was stone, probably quartz or granite, and no bigger than an egg. This one had required time.

By now, I had more than a hundred of them and always a new one to welcome me home when I've been away.

Birds and a happy beagle we called Matilde.

"Hello there," I said as she tap danced at my feet. "Have you been good?"

She let out an indignant howl and I crouched down to receive my ration of kisses and irritable *where have you been?* yips.

"She's been hunting badgers again," Gus called as he shuffled down the stairs. From my position on the floor, I couldn't see him but I loved the sleepy drawl in his voice and the lazy way he thudded from one riser to the next. Sleepy, lazy Gus was one of my favorite iterations of this man. "She thinks it's her duty to thin the local population."

I gifted Matilde a meaningful stare. "Again?" She replied by nestling her head against my belly and frantically wagging her whole tail end. It was never just the tail. Always the whole back half of her body, wagging like it was making a wide turn.

"I tried to reason with her, particularly with respect to her commitment to leaving her trophies under the deck," he continued, stepping into the kitchen with both palms pressed to his eyes, "but she wasn't having it. She said it was her life's work and who am I to argue with that?"

I took Matilde's face in my hands, melting at her contagiously joyful grin. "We're not getting the hunter out of you, are we?"

"Owen appreciates it," Gus said, stopping behind me. "When I dropped by for dinner last night, he told me the badgers were gnawing on some of his nets last month. Digging up some of his cucumber plants too. Cole told me a long story about the Canadian fur trade. I don't remember the specifics. I was busy drinking his gin."

I gained my feet and stepped into his space, my arms closing around his lean—and delightfully bare—torso. He was still busy waking up, his skin warm and hair sticking in every direction, and he was mine.

"It seems I should ask whether *you've* been good?" I pressed my lips to my husband's neck. *Husband.* And I was his wife. Even after two years of marriage, that title still caught me like a blast of blinding sunshine after a week of dreary darkness. Of all the titles I'd collected in my life, *wife* wasn't one I'd expected. But now, I couldn't imagine living without it.

We'd stumbled into the nuptial conversation around the time Gus was finishing his residency back in Silicon Valley. Nothing about that year had been easy on us. I still couldn't believe we'd made it out intact. He'd moved himself into my apartment immediately following our return from Talbott's Cove, though neither of us were skilled at the art of cohabitation. We argued—*a lot*—and gradually learned the difference between disagreeing about issues of importance and instigating in the name of foreplay. Very, very gradually.

Once I'd announced my intention to step away from the company, my business travel schedule quadrupled as I was busy transitioning projects and management tasks at locations all over the globe. Even when I was in the office, my days started before sunrise and ended long past sunset, leaving us little time for both disagreement and instigation. Save for the weeks scheduled for visiting Talbott's Cove, I saw more of Gus's carved birds than I did of him during that period.

Thankfully, he'd discovered life beyond the stiff boundaries of the Valley and spent most of his time exploring everything from Big Sur to Half Dome. He'd stayed as far away from the campus as possible and, in that time, managed to create several spectacular sculptures which were now on display in the campus's flagship building. He'd claimed they were the worst thing he'd made since primary school. I disagreed but I loved him enough to know when to argue, when to instigate, and when to let him be wrong without telling him about it.

In addition to all the drama and exhaustion of that year, and our plan to move into a renovated farmhouse on the other side of the country, we'd decided to get married. The idea had first come up when Gus mentioned his O1-B visa was expiring and he was due to apply for an extension unless I'd rather save him the time and marry him.

We'd laughed for a minute because he hadn't meant to propose. He hadn't. Not after the year of constant bickering and separation and frustration over one thing or another. There were days when we barely tolerated each other and required some angry sex in semi-public locations to break through the tension. There were days when we doubted our plan to build a new life together in Maine because how could we do that when we couldn't agree on whether to run the ceiling fan all night, regardless of the weather. But I stopped laughing and I set all those issues aside, and I said, "Yes, I'd like that very much."

Two weeks later, we flew to Talbott's Cove. Owen conducted a brief ceremony in the forest which ended with, "I now pronounce you husband and wife. You may now adopt a dog."

None of these things were part of our plans but now, a little more than two years after our impromptu wedding, I couldn't imagine life without my husband and our heart-of-a-killer dog. The learning curve was steep but we'd scaled it together.

We still argued, still instigated. Still engaged in angry sex in semi-public places. But our world was different now and we didn't need the same things.

"I've never once been good." Gus slipped his hand down my back to squeeze my ass. He smelled like oil paint and pine needles, which meant he'd been painting in the barn. Unlike his former studio back in California, the barn was nothing more than a barn. Wooden beams, dirt floors, a single string of lightbulbs running down the center. The ocean-facing front was almost always bathed in bright sun, the forest-facing back was almost always shaded under the branches of old pines. It was uncomfortably simple and exactly the way he preferred to work. "How could I possibly start now? I wouldn't know where to begin."

"An excellent point." I dropped my cheek to his chest and inhaled. "Was the late night courtesy of the gin or the paint?"

"Gin, then paint," he replied, bringing his hand to the back of my neck and kneading the tense muscles there. Leaving Silicon Valley and launching a strategic philanthropy venture was exciting—and stressful as hell. Making the decisions *and* executing them kept my days busy and my hands full, though I savored this stress. I'd chosen it and I was the one to plot the course. "How was Cape Town?"

"Intense, but good." I hummed as his thumb found an especially tough knot. "More of that, please."

"More you shall receive," he murmured. "Tired, sparrow?"

I kicked my shoes off, shook my head. "Not right now. I took a nap on the flight."

"Good thinking." He edged my feet apart as he kneaded his thumbs down my back. I heard the rustle of fabric and felt his pajama bottoms drop to the floor. His hard cock slapped my belly, hot and hungry for attention. He dragged his stubbled chin over my neck, between the open collar of my blouse. "But you'll be tired when I'm finished with you."

Matilde slunk off to the sunny guest bedroom she'd claimed as her own while Gus freed me from my clothing. His fingertips drew patterns up and down my spine, and then lower, over my ass, slipping inside me.

"Miz Malik," he growled. "Oh, my beautiful girl. You are wet like the ocean."

"I have been away for nineteen days," I replied.

He offered another growl as he turned me, wrapping his arms around my waist, and walked me toward the living room, his cock nestled between my ass cheeks. A two-story wall of windows showcased all of Talbott's Cove and Penobscot Bay. He gathered several pillows from the sofa as we passed, tossing them to the floor in front of the window.

"Down," he ordered with a gentle shove.

I dropped to the floor and settled my knees on the pillows I'd selected for this precise purpose—but no one else had to know that. Gus joined me, an arm tight around my waist as he layered his body over mine. His erection slid through my slit and the early spasms of release danced up my legs, circled my ribs, prickled my scalp. *I am so ready for this.* When he finally thrust inside me, his cock gloriously thick and heavy, our cries echoed in the cavernous space.

"Your cunt missed me something fierce." He fisted my hair, angling my head to drag his teeth over my neck. "Did you play with it while you were gone? Did you open the curtains in your suite and spread your legs and tease this little clit until you came?"

"Once or twice," I replied.

Gus released my hair and reached down, slapping my mound as he slammed into me. "More than that," he said. Slapped again, and again. His chest tightened against my back, his muscles pulled taut, his breaths coming fast, his control eroding with each measured stroke. "More than that, sparrow."

"Did you miss me?" I asked.

He didn't answer right away, only delivering another fast, sharp slap between my legs. Then, "The next time you're alone in a hotel room with your legs spread, I expect a phone call. I want to hear it happening."

Gus pumped into me, his fingers swirling around my clit as he sucked my neck. "That can be arranged."

"Neera," he said, groaning. "Oh, fuck, I—*fuuuuck.*"

"Yes," I panted. "Tell me."

"You should've woken me up by sitting on my face."

"Next time," I promised.

"I fucking love you," he snarled. He came with a hoarse shout and his teeth on my shoulder, and I followed. We stayed there, quaking, panting, and I wanted this little moment to last forever.

"I love you too," I whispered.

He pulled out, and slapped my ass. "Welcome home, sparrow."

———

THANK **you for reading *Rough Sketch!* I hope you enjoyed Neera and Gus. Keep reading for a sneak peek of JJ and Brooke's story—*Far Cry*!**

"MY TAVERN ISN'T your hookup pool."

She cast her gaze from one end of the bar to the other. "I wouldn't call it much of a pool."

"Why can't you use Tinder like everyone else? Come on, sweetheart. Get yourself some apps and get the hell outta here."

"I hate apps," she replied.

"And I hate cilantro, but you don't see me passing on the tacos, do you?"

"No, I mean I *hate* apps," she said, holding up her phone. "I hate them so much that I don't have any." I snatched the device away from her and peered at the screen. "Look. No social media. No news or weather. No food delivery."

"The only delivery around here is DiLorenzo's and it's only when Denny's in the mood."

She sliced her hands through the air. "Irrelevant. I didn't have delivery apps when I lived in New York."

I hit her with a glare. "If you really wanted something, you'd download an app for it."

"And that's where you're wrong, Jed. If I really wanted something, I'd go out and get it." She waved her hands. "That's what I was attempting to do earlier."

I set her phone on the bar top. "You have the newest iPhone and you use it for what? Phone calls? Texting Annette?"

She tilted her head, schooling me with an expression that said I should know better. "Not that I owe you any kind of explanation but until recently, when my previous phone met with an unlikely end, I had one of the earliest models." She pursed her lips. I looked away to keep from staring at her there. "And yes, Jed, I use it to make phone calls and text my bloodless sister."

I blew out a breath as I reached for towel. All the glass-ware was dry, but goddamn, I needed something to keep my hands busy. "You come out with a lot of strange shit, BamBam, but that's the strangest."

"It's so great that you have opinions," she mused. "Even better that I don't give a single fuck what you think." She leaned forward, folded her arms on the lip of the bar. "Then again, I can't give a single fuck because I don't have any. Literally. I have no fucks because you cockblocked me."

"What d'you want from me, Brooke? An apology? You're not getting one. I kicked the guy out because he annoyed me. When you own the joint, you can do that."

"You kicked him out while also cockblocking me," she replied.

"Not that it'd matter to you, but I'm pretty sure he's married."

"'Not that it'd matter to you,'" she repeated. "Your dick isn't big enough to use that tone of voice with me. Check yourself, Jed."

"Sweetheart, you don't know the first thing about my dick."

Her blonde hair spilled over her shoulders as she leaned forward. "Oh, I know more than enough."

I twisted the towel around my fist. "Big talk from a girl trying to pick up tourists."

"Funny how it's only a problem when I do it."

I blinked at her. Dropped the towel. Swallowed down the words I wanted to say to her. Rounded the bar. I closed my hand around Brooke's bicep and tugged her off the stool. "Let's go," I murmured.

"And where, may I ask, are we going?"

I gave her only a clenched jaw in response as I yanked her around the bar and into the dim storeroom. I kicked the door shut behind us. I marched her toward a wall of empty kegs until her back met the cool metal.

"Excuse you," she said, glaring at my hold on her arm. "What do you think you're doing with your hand on me?"

"We both know you would've ripped my fucking ear off and kicked my balls into my gut by now if you didn't want my hand on you."

"Oh really?" she scoffed. "So, what? I'm *asking for it?*"

"You're asking for something, sweetheart."

I was right about that. She was looking for something. She was fishing.

And I was taking the bait.

FAR CRY IS NOW AVAILABLE!

Join Kate Canterbary's Office Memos mailing list for occasional news and updates, as well as new release alerts, exclusive extended epilogues and bonus scenes, and cake. There's always cake.

Visit Kate's private reader group to chat about books, get early peeks at new books, and hang out with over booklovers!

If newsletters aren't your jam, follow Kate on BookBub for preorder and new release alerts.

Talbott's Cove

Fresh Catch — Owen and Cole

Hard Pressed — Jackson and Annette

Far Cry — Brooke and JJ

Rough Sketch — Gus and Neera

Benchmarks Series

Professional Development — Drew and Tara

Orientation — Jory and Max

Brothers In Arms

Missing In Action — Wes and Tom

Coastal Elite — Jordan and April

Get exclusive sneak previews of upcoming releases through Kate's newsletter and private reader group, The Canterbary Tales, on Facebook.

acknowledgments

This book—like most others from me—is the product of mulling ideas for months and years. It's also the product of cheerleading and support from dear friends, author colleagues, and eager readers. You know who you are and you know how you've helped me, and for that, I'm forever thankful.

Many thanks to the Read Me Romance podcast and narrators Savannah Peachwood and Christian Fox for introducing the world to Neera and Gus.

Now and always, gratitude goes out to all the pervy girls from Kate Canterbary's Tales. Your love and affection for these characters astounds me every day.

My husband doesn't read my books but he does flip to the back to see if he's been mentioned in the acknowledgements. So, here you go, honey. Thank you for keeping the coffee flowing and only asking when I'd be finished with this one a few times.